Take a rich old lady – preferably for every penny she's got. Not a bad scheme. But how? Take her for a ride – preferably as her chauffeur. Infiltrate a partner in crime as her companion, make the old girl's will the target, and you've got a chance of landing over one million bucks. It's just a matter of time . . .

By the same author

JAMES HADLEY CHASE

Just a Matter of Time

GRAFTON BOOKS

A Division of the Collins Publishing Group

LONDON GLASGOW
TORONTO SYDNEY AUCKLAND

Grafton Books
A Division of the Collins Publishing Group
8 Grafton Street, London W1X 3LA

Published by Grafton Books 1973
Reprinted 1975, 1977, 1978, 1980 (twice), 1984,
1986, 1989

First published in Great Britain by
Robert Hale & Co 1972

Copyright © James Hadley Chase 1972

ISBN 0-586-03782-9

Printed and bound in Great Britain by
Collins, Glasgow

Set in Linotype Plantin

One

Patterson looked up from a list of Stock quotations lying on his desk as Bailey came in.

'What is it now, Joe?' he asked impatiently. 'Not another one?'

'That's it, Mr Patterson ... another one.' Bailey's fat face lit up with a leering grin and he closed a heavy eyelid. 'You won't want to miss this one, Mr Patterson,' and pursing his thick lips, he released a soft whistle.

Patterson leaned back in his padded leather chair. He was a tall, athletically built man in his early thirties and very aware of his good looks. His numerous girl-friends had told him that he reminded them of David Niven, the movie star when Niven had been young, and Patterson was inclined to agree, but he had resisted the urge to grow a pencil-lined moustache now that the modern trend was all hair.

'What's the wink for, Joe?' he demanded, his voice hostile.

'Wink, sir? No wink ... I've got something in my eye.' Bailey stiffened at the snap in Patterson's voice, remembering that although Patterson was all charm when dealing with the bank's clients, he could be a sonofabitch with the staff. 'Miss Sheila Oldhill waiting, sir.'

Patterson hesitated. He had promised Bernie Cohen an early analysis of his portfolio with suggestions for growth, but Mrs Morely-Johnson's need for a companion-help took precedence. After all, he thought, there were dozens of Bernie Cohens, but only one Mrs Morely-Johnson.

'I'll see her,' he said, pushing aside the papers littering his desk. As Bailey made for the door, Patterson went on, 'And get that thing out of your eye. It could create a wrong impression.'

Bastard! Bailey thought as he said, 'Yes, sir.'

Patterson pulled a file towards him, opened it and studied his scribbled notes. He had interviewed five elderly women this morning. Four of them had been unsatisfactory, but the fifth, Mrs Madge Fleming, seemed acceptable. Aged fifty-three, she was a stout, cheerful, quietly spoken woman who was willing to please. She had impeccable references and had been for some fifteen years a companion-help to a wealthy widow who had recently died and now she was looking for another such appointment. Patterson, utterly bored with this chore, had almost

5

decided to engage her, subject, of course to Mrs Morely-Johnson's approval, but he felt that he had to give Mrs Morely-Johnson a second choice and he had told Mrs Fleming to stand by in readiness for an interview.

He became aware that a woman had come into his office and he looked up, his head a little on one side, his left eyebrow raised, his right forefinger pressing on the dimple in his chin. He had cultivated this pose before his bathroom mirror and he now felt it gave him the confident, nonchalant air of an up-and-coming Bank executive.

As Bailey closed the door behind her, the woman moved further into the room and Patterson, regarding her, felt a tingle creep up his spine. He got to his feet, immediately understanding Bailey's leer and wink.

'Miss Oldhill?' He waved to a chair. 'Please sit down.'

He watched her move to the chair and settle herself. Her movements were unhurried, graceful and calm. She was tall: her shoulders square and her raven black hair glossy. She was not what he would call pretty nor beautiful, but there was a compelling handsomeness in the Grecian nose, the big, smoky blue eyes and the large, firm mouth. But all this wasn't what sent a hot wave of blood through him. This woman exuded a magnetic sensuality that was like a hundred-watt lamp flimsily concealed by a Cashmere shawl. He could see this as Bailey had seen it, and yet by her calmness and by the way she was looking directly at him without any sign of self-consciousness he couldn't be sure if she was aware of it or not: this intrigued him.

Looking at her as he sat down, he thought she was thirty or possibly thirty-two years of age. He looked swiftly at her clothes: inexpensive, in fashion and neat: the skirt an inch above the knee. He couldn't see her legs from where he was sitting but he felt instinctively they would be exciting and good-looking.

He abruptly realized his examination was causing an awkward pause and he jerked his mind back to business.

'You have come in answer to our advertisement?' he asked, picking up his gold pencil, an expensive Christmas gift from Mrs Morely-Johnson, and pulling a scratch pad towards him.

'Yes.'

By leaning forward slightly, he could see her knees were pressed together and her hands rested on a black leather handbag. He became aware of her hands. The long tapering fingers and the narrow back of her hands were, to him, sensual. The thought of those hands moving over his body made him shift in his chair.

'You couldn't have read it very carefully,' he said and smiled. He was pleased with his smile, knowing his teeth were excellent and his smile radiated warmth. 'We are advertising for an elderly woman, Miss Oldhill ... you can scarcely call yourself that.'

She regarded him steadily, her chin up, her smoky blue eyes remote.

'I wouldn't have thought, these days, being elderly is a qualification for any job,' she said quietly. 'But if you really are looking for an elderly woman then I won't take up any more of your time.'

They looked at each other and he noted she made no move to get up. He was thinking: She's sensational! What a lay she would be! He looked down at his scratch pad suddenly uneasy that she might read from the expression in his eyes what was going through his mind.

'You could be right,' he said and began to dig holes in his blotter with the point of his pencil. 'This is rather out of my field.' Feeling now in control himself, he looked up and smiled. 'My client is used to an elderly companion. The woman she has had for the past ten years has died rather suddenly and my client is in urgent need of a replacement.' He paused, glancing at the still figure, then went on, 'I don't know how she would react to someone as young as you.'

Sheila Oldhill remained still, her eyes looking directly into his and he looked away. As she said nothing, he went on, 'But it might be an idea. She might be glad to have someone around as young as you ... it might be an idea.'

Again the polite silence: again the steady look.

Seeing he was spoiling the appearance of his blotter, he laid down his pencil.

'You've read the advertisement,' he said, leaning back and forcing himself to relax. 'We want a capable woman to act as companion-help for one of our clients. You might think it odd for a bank to handle such a – a chore, shall I say? But this particular client is important and I do all kinds of chores for her.'

Sheila nodded. Still no body movement, still the faint, quizzing expression in the smoky blue eyes.

'What makes you think you would be suitable for such a job?'

he asked, determined to make her talk.

'If you will explain what the duties would be, I would be able to give you an intelligent answer,' she said.

There was even a sensual caress in her voice, he thought, as he again picked up his pencil to dig holes in the blotter.

'My client is seventy-eight years old and proud of it,' he said. 'She is very wealthy and lives in a penthouse suite at the best hotel here. She has a cataract on both eyes and is half blind. She has a horror of operations and refuses to have her eyes fixed. She needs a sympathetic type of woman to live with her to take care of her daily needs such as answering letters, reading the newspapers to her, helping her dress, going to the shops with her ... that sort of thing. She is easy to live with, kind, considerate and in no way tiresome. The hotel staff look after the penthouse. She has a chauffeur. Apart from being half blind, she is in no way helpless.'

'Then I think I can be of use,' Sheila said without hesitation. 'I am a trained nurse. I was at the Pendick Foundation Hospital, New York, for four years. Previously, I was nurse-secretary to Dr Gordon Fosdick, a leading surgeon in Washington. I do fast shorthand and typing. I drive a car. I speak good French and I am musical.'

Patterson made notes.

'This sounds fine,' he said. 'Not that Mrs Morely-Johnson needs nursing, but one never knows at her age.' He leaned back in his chair and regarded her. 'But surely, Miss Oldhill, if you are a trained nurse with these extra qualifications, you could get something more interesting than being a companion to an old lady?'

She stared down at her handbag for a brief moment, then looked at him.

'I suppose I could, but I am very tired. The last four years have been hard. I like this city. Perhaps you don't realize how strenuous hospital life can be, Mr Patterson.' So she had got his name, Patterson thought and was flattered. 'If I could find something less strenuous, it would be helpful. You see I used to play the violin. I have a muscle condition in my bowing arm. I've been told that it will come right, providing I don't do strenuous work, then I can begin playing again.'

Patterson lifted his left eyebrow.

'You are a violinist?'

'I was. I just wasn't good enough to become a professional so I took up nursing, but the violin is my first love. My father was

8

first violinist with the New York Philharmonic. Music runs in my family.'

Patterson drew in a long, slow breath.

'Being a musician is a better qualification than being a trained nurse, Miss Oldhill. Before she married, Mrs Morely-Johnson was Alice Lesson, the concert pianist. You have probably heard of her?'

Sheila Oldhill nodded.

'Of course. She was as good as Myra Hess. She once played with my father.'

'Quite a coincidence. You understand as she is half blind she plays the piano a lot. It's her way of passing the time. She might welcome you as a fellow-musician.' He regarded her calm face. 'You say she played with your father?'

'It was twenty-five years ago. She played the Beethoven Emperor. It was my first concert, and the first time I had seen my father on a concert platform.'

'What was your father's name?'

'Henry Oldhill.'

'Is he alive? Mrs Morely-Johnson is certain to ask.'

'He died three years ago.'

'Have you been here long, Miss Oldhill?'

'I arrived two days ago. I was on my way to Los Angeles, but I liked this city and decided to stop off for a few days. I am staying at the Franklin Hotel and saw your advertisement. I wondered...' She paused.

Patterson knew the Franklin Hotel. It was sedate and reasonably cheap: not the kind of place he would have liked to stay in, but then he had high standards.

'This is very interesting,' he said. 'I would like to take up your references. You understand, of course, I have the responsibility of finding someone suitable for Mrs Morely-Johnson. I don't know you ... as you don't know me.' He gave her his warm smile. 'Have you a reference ...' he paused to look at his notes '... from Dr Fosdick?'

She looked directly at him. Her smoky blue eyes opened a little and he found her even more exciting.

'No, but I have a reference from the Pendick Foundation Hospital.' She opened her handbag and took from it an envelope which she put on the desk.

He read the reference. It was impersonal and signed by one of the Hospital Governors. It said that Sheila Oldhill, a qualified nurse, had been with them for four years and had always been a hard worker, honest, trustworthy and good with patients. It wasn't a rave reference, but it was adequate.

'Could I call Dr Fosdick if you haven't a reference from him?' Patterson asked.

'Dr Fosdick wouldn't give me a reference,' she said as she looked directly at him.

Patterson lifted his left eyebrow.

'He wouldn't? Why not?'

'He would be prejudiced.' She hesitated, then went on, 'He tried to become familiar with me. There was an unpleasant scene and I had to leave.'

Patterson picked up his pencil and began to dig more holes in his blotter. He could imagine the situation: a doctor working under pressure, closeted all day with this sexy woman. He, himself, would have tried a pass if he had been in the same position. He couldn't imagine any normal man not doing so. But she had walked out and that told him she was no pushover, but then he hadn't seen Fosdick. He could be old, fat and ugly.

'I understand.' He was now a little dubious. This was his responsibility. He mustn't make a mistake. Yet he wanted this woman to get the job. He wanted to see her again. At least three times a week he had to visit Mrs Morely-Johnson and that would mean he would be able to see Shcila Oldhill at least three times a week, and this, he realized, was what he wanted. There was this sensual thing in this woman who was sitting so quietly that set him on fire. Compared to the other women he had known, loved and forgotten, she was like a 1929 Claret compared to a Coke.

Women played an important role in Patterson's life. Being assistant manager of the bank and living in this small, gossip-ridden city, he was always careful and selective. Most of the women he went with lived in the adjacent town, some fifteen miles from his home town and all of them were married. They had to be as careful as he. His thoughts were so far away that for a moment he had forgotten her when he was aware she had said something. He looked up.

'Sorry ... I was thinking ... what did you say?'

'Perhaps you don't think I am suitable?' she repeated.

They looked at each other.

'I think you are, but I just don't know how Mrs Morely-Johnson will react when I tell her you are so young. How old are you, if I may ask?'

'Thirty-two.'

'Would you mind if I told her you are thirty-eight?' He smiled. 'It could make a difference and you see ... she doesn't see very well.'

'I don't mind.'

He wished she would smile. She was so serious, quiet and calm.

'I tell you what I will do. I have to see her this afternoon. I'll explain who you are and so on. If she's interested I'll arrange for you to see her some time tomorrow. How's that?'

A faint sparkle came into the smoky blue eyes and the firm lips curved into something Patterson thought was a smile: whatever it was he liked it.

'Thank you, Mr Patterson,' she said and got to her feet.

He looked at the tall, firmly built body and again he felt the surge of blood run through him.

'I hope I can fix it. I think I can.' He got to his feet. 'You haven't asked what the pay would be.'

She began to move slowly to the door.

'I am sure it will be adequate. I'd rather not be told until I know the job is mine.' She reached the door and put her hand on the door knob. 'That way I won't be disappointed.'

He came around the desk and approached her.

'As soon as I know I'll tell you,' he said. 'Will you be at your hotel say around seven o'clock?'

'I could be.'

'I pass your hotel on my way home ... suppose I look in?'

'If you haven't any good news for me then I won't expect you.'

'I'll drop by ... good or bad news. I think it will be good.'

She studied him in her calm remote way, nodded, turned, opened the door and walked out into the busy stream of people passing up and down the broad aisle of the bank.

Patterson closed the door. He stood for a long moment staring down at the thick green pile of the carpet, pressing his forefinger against his dimple, then he walked back to his desk, sat down and drew Bernie Cohen's portfolio towards him.

The long list of securities and bonds meant nothing to him. He could only see the smoky blue eyes and that firm mouth floating on the page. He sat there for half an hour doing nothing but thinking of her, then seeing the time, he shoved the portfolio into a drawer in his desk, got to his feet and left the bank.

He drove fast towards the Plaza Beach Hotel.

Seaview Boulevard began in luxury and slowly deteriorated as it wound its way along the coast to mediocrity and then finally to slum conditions. The boulevard was two miles long. It began with the Plaza Beach Hotel with its own private beach, gay sun umbrellas, a thatched roof bar and restaurant, its boutiques and a jeweller's shop whose windows blazed with diamonds. Several yards further on, past an ornamental public garden with tropical flowers and graceful palm trees was the Splendid Hotel, not quite so grand as the Plaza Beach but still expensive and with a smaller private beach. Further on still was the Ambassador Hotel which had no private beach and its frontage needed a coat of paint. Then came the tourist shops and also further deterioration. A mile from the Plaza Beach was the Franklin Hotel, strictly a family hotel, inexpensive, shabby but comfortable. Beyond the Franklin was the harbour and the fishermen's huts, bars, cheap sea-food restaurants, and still further on were the tenement blocks housing those who scratched up some kind of living along the waterfront.

Gerald Hammett sat on the balcony that ran the length of the Franklin Hotel and watched the fishing boats and the bustle of the harbour with bored indifference. From time to time he glanced at his cheap wrist-watch with an impatient frown.

Gerald Hammett was twenty-six years of age, slimly built, his blond hair resting on the collar of his red and white striped shirt, open at the neck. His carefully cultivated sideboards like right angle triangles with the peaks at his ears and the bases reaching the corners of his mouth linked up with a thick, droopy moustache, gave him a slightly sinister appearance. His eyes were small, steel grey and restless; his mouth thin, his nose short and blunt. He looked what he was: a typical product of instability, dissatisfied with his way of life, groping, not knowing what he wanted, unsure of himself but with a latent viciousness that could be sparked off should he encounter any kind of opposition or criticism.

Carrying a shabby hold-all, he had arrived at the hotel the previous evening. Sheila Oldhill had been in the lounge, but they had been careful not to look at each other. As he passed her, she traced with her finger on the open page of her novel the figure 3, telling him she was booked in on the third floor. The hotel was half empty and he had no difficulty getting a room on the third floor. He engaged the room for a week and added he might need it longer. The reception clerk said it would be their pleasure and personally conducted him to the room.

Sheila and Hammett had agreed it wouldn't be safe for them to be seen together. After midnight when the rest of the people staying at the hotel were asleep and only the Negro night porter dozed in the lobby, Hammett had slipped from his room, crossed the corridor and slid into Sheila's room. There, they had sat on the bed and had talked in low whispers. Although he wanted to stay longer, she wouldn't let him and this put him in a surly mood. He had spent an uneasy night wondering about this plan, if she would succeed and wishing he hadn't agreed to go along with her. But he wanted her ... he needed her and he knew if he wanted to keep her, he had to co-operate.

She had left the hotel when Hammett had come down to breakfast and he had spent the morning wandering around the town. It was a nice town, but it quickly bored him. He was short of money (when wasn't he?) and it irked him not to be able to go into the Plaza Beach Hotel bar and having to make do with a Coke in a sleazy waterfront bar crammed with sweaty, loud-mouthed fishermen.

He had returned to the Franklin for a poor lunch and had now been sitting on the balcony for the past two hours. Sheila had said she would be back by 16.00. It was now 16.20 and there was still no sign of her.

He took from his hip pocket a thin roll of dollar bills and furtively counted them. They amounted to $55. Sheila had about the same amount. If she didn't pull this off, he thought, they would have to move fast. With the prices as they were in this luxury tourist trap, a hundred dollars would last no time.

Then he saw her as she came along the wide sidewalk and he felt his heartbeat quicken. He couldn't judge from her expression whether she had been successful or not. She always looked the same: calm, quiet and remote, and this often infuriated him. Even when she was angry with him, she always remained calm, only the tone of her voice sharpened and the smoky blue eyes became more alive.

Without hurrying, she came up the steps leading to the lobby and went past him without looking at him. He felt a surge of exasperated rage rush through him and he had to restrain himself from jumping to his feet and going after her. She was like an iceberg, he thought. Nothing ever moved her! She must know how the past hours had dragged for him! Couldn't she have given him just a slight hint of success as she had gone by?

He looked around and through the dirty window and into the

lobby. She was standing at the reception desk, waiting for the old Negro clerk to give her her key. Again Hammett had to restrain himself from getting up. He fumbled for a cigarette and with an unsteady hand he struck a match and lit the cigarette. He looked at his chewed finger-nails and the yellow nicotine stains on his slender fingers and he grimaced.

He sat there for five long, nerve-tearing minutes, then forcing himself to act casually, he got to his feet and wandered into the lobby.

There were four or five elderly people sitting in ancient bamboo chairs, gossiping and he was aware the hum of their voices died as he crossed the lobby.

Get stuffed, you old ruins, he thought. Go, climb into your goddam coffins!

'Room thirty-two,' he said, coming to rest at the reception desk.

'Yes, sir. Thirty-two it is, sir.'

A gnarled black hand slid the key across the scratched surface of the desk.

'Would you be in for dinner tonight, sir?' The old Negro beamed at him. 'It's a good dinner. I've seen it. Soup, nice fried fish and ice cream.' There was a yearning note in his voice as if he longed to have this for himself.

Hammett winced. He had no alternative but to take the dinner. He was there on full pension which offered the cheapest rates.

'I'll be there,' he said and picking up his key, he made his way towards the ancient elevator.

He walked along the deserted corridor of the third floor, paused outside his room, looked right and left, then moved swiftly to Sheila's room, two doors further down the corridor. He turned the handle, felt the door yield and slid into the room shutting the door softly behind him.

Sheila was standing before the open window. She had on a transparent cotton wrap. With the light against her, he could see her long, shapely legs and the curve of her firm buttocks through the flimsy material. This sight always affected him, but this wasn't the time for such feelings.

She looked around, then aware he was staring, she moved to a chair and sat down. It was the only chair in the room, a sagging thing that creaked under the weight of her body.

'I asked you not to come here until after midnight,' she said quietly. 'Can't you ever do what I ask?'

He sat on the bed.

'It's all right. There's no one up here. What happened?'

'We must wait and see. At least, I know now he is on my side.'

Hammett frowned.

'You mean Jack was right? He's got this creep lined up?'

'I think so.'

The flat note in her voice made him look sharply at her.

'What's biting you? Why are you looking so goddamed depressed?'

'Am I?'

'Oh, for God's sake! Is something wrong?'

She looked directly at him.

'Not so far. It just isn't settled yet. They want an elderly woman. He said he would try to persuade her, but that doesn't mean he will.'

Hammett ran his fingers through his dirty hair.

'So what? He'll persuade her. Jack says she has the hots for him. Anything this creep says goes with her.'

'An old woman of seventy-eight?'

Hammett grinned.

'I know my aunt. She has always had the hots for men like this creep ... suave, sexy and handsome. She has never been able to resist them. If Jack says she has the hots for this guy Patterson that's what she's got, so what Patterson says will be okay with her.'

Sheila leaned back in her chair.

'How stupid can you be?' she said quietly. She crossed her long legs, adjusting her wrap. 'He sees a lot of her. A woman like that would want always to be the centre of attraction. She might not care to have a young woman around who might catch Patterson's eye. Now, do you understand why I'm doubtful?'

Hammett began to chew his thumbnail.

'So what? I keep telling you ... I don't like this. Let's get out of this stinking town. Let's go to L.A.'

'Patterson said he would tell her I am thirty-eight,' Sheila went on ignoring what he had said. 'He knows the danger, but even thirty-eight could be too young. She could kill this stone dead.'

'All right ... so she kills it! I ...'

'Be quiet, Gerry!'

'Oh, the hell with it! Let's get out of here!'

Sheila glanced at her wrist-watch.

'Patterson is coming here when he has seen her. I want to

take a shower. I think he is going to take me out to dinner. He said he would drop by whether the news was good or bad. Run along, Gerry. I have to dress.'

He stared sullenly at her, then moved to the door. As he turned the handle, he paused, looking at her.

'Sometimes I think I'm crazy in the head to have hooked up with you,' he said savagely. 'Do you have to be so goddamn cold-blooded ... like a goddamn Mona Lisa?'

'Run along, please. I want to change,' she said after staring at him for a brief moment, then moving past him, she went into the shower room.

As Patterson pulled up outside the Franklin Hotel in his red Wildcat coupé, he saw Sheila Oldhill sitting on the veranda and he waved to her. She got to her feet and came down the steps as he slid out of the car, holding the off-side door open. It was nearing 20.00 and everyone, including Hammett, was in the dining-room.

Patterson's eyes went over her as she crossed the sidewalk. She wore a simple white dress with a gilt chain around her slim waist and she carried a white plastic handbag. He thought she looked terrific.

'Hello,' he said with his warm smile. 'There's lots to talk about. Will you please have dinner with me? I'm starving, and as I said ... there's lots to talk about.'

Her smoky blue eyes opened a trifle wider. She appeared to hesitate, then she nodded.

'Thank you. Yes, I would like to.'

'Then hop in. Do you like sea food?'

'I like anything.' She got into the car, careful with her skirt. She showed Patterson only her knees as he closed the door.

Patterson got in beside her. Obviously, she thought, he had been home for he was freshly shaven and was wearing a dark suit and a fresh shirt. She could smell his after-shave lotion.

'I think it's going to be all right,' he said as he edged the car into the heavy evening traffic. 'There are things we have to talk about, but right now, it looks good. Everything will depend on you from now on.'

'Yes.' She leaned back in the comfortable seat. 'It is very kind of you, Mr Patterson, to take so much trouble.'

'Oh, I'm an interested party.' He laughed. 'I have to see Mrs Morely-Johnson quite a lot. There are certain chores I had to discuss with her late companion. It wasn't much fun as she didn't approve of me.' He laughed again. 'You and I, I hope, could get along together.'

'Yes.'

He glanced at her. She was looking through the windshield at the red tail-lights of the cars ahead of them. The line of her throat stirred him. He imagined holding her, his mouth pressed against that lovely firm flesh. From past experiences he knew women reacted violently when he kissed their throats.

He slowed and turned off the boulevard.

'We're just here. This is my favourite restaurant. Not only is the food good but the doorman takes care of the car.'

He pulled up outside a doorway over which was a blue and gold canopy. The doorman, dressed in blue and gold, opened the off-side door, lifting his peak cap.

'Evening, Mr Patterson. Evening, miss.'

'Hi, Fred! Take her away, will you, please?' Patterson got out of the car and came around as Sheila got out. He put his hand possessively on her arm and led her into the restaurant. Ahead of them, down a short corridor, she could see the crowded restaurant, but Patterson guided her towards a narrow flight of stairs. 'Up you go,' he said. 'We're on the first floor.'

At the head of the stairs, a smiling *maître d'hôtel* was waiting, a bunch of leather menus under his arm.

'Evening, Mr Patterson ... ma'am.' Shiela was aware of his sharp scrutiny, then seeing his smile broaden, she knew he approved of her. 'This way, please.'

He opened a door and ushered them into a small room containing a table set for two, two red and gilt plush chairs, the walls covered with red plush and before the curtained window a broad red plush settee.

'Two champagne cocktails, Henry,' Patterson said. 'Right away.'

'Certainly, Mr Patterson,' and the *maître d'hôtel* vanished.

Sheila looked around the room, eyed the settee, turned and looked at the door, noting there was a brass bolt to it.

'I didn't know such places still existed,' she said.

Patterson pulled out one of the chairs from the table and waved her to it.

'Not many ... I use this place quite a bit for business.' He smiled. 'It always makes an impression and the bank pays.'

As she sat down, she looked directly at him.

'Will the bank be paying tonight?'

He laughed as he sat down.

'No ... this is my pleasure. Do you like oysters?'

'Yes ... very much.'

The *maître d'hôtel* returned, followed by a waiter bearing two champagne cocktails.

She sat back and watched Patterson glance at the menu. He was quietly efficient and she could see he could quickly make up his mind. Without consulting her further, he ordered nine oysters each and the fish pie.

'The usual white wine, Mr Patterson?' the *maître d'hôtel* asked.

Patterson nodded. When they were alone, he said, 'Fish pie might sound dull, but here it is good ... their speciality: lobster tails, mussels and shrimps in a white wine sauce, covered by the lightest pastry and served with fonds d'artichauts. Sound all right?'

'It sounds wonderful.'

He raised his glass.

'Here's to your success.'

Without touching her glass, she looked directly at him.

'Mr Patterson, do you always treat companion-helps this way?'

Patterson lifted his left eyebrow, smiling.

'This is the first time I've tried to engage a companion-help,' he said. 'So you have me at a disadvantage. The answer, I suppose, is that it depends on the companion-help.'

She picked up her glass, sipped, then put it down.

'You think I have a chance?'

'Yes ... a good chance.' He drank half his cocktail, then went on, 'But when dealing with old people you can never be sure. In confidence, I have quite a time with the old lady when she is in the wrong mood, but she was in the right mood this evening ... the snag is she could be in the wrong mood by tomorrow.'

The oysters arrived on a silver tray of crushed ice. While the waiter fussed with lemons, Tabasco and bread, they said nothing. When he had gone, Patterson went on, 'The trouble is, Miss Oldhill, she's a bit worried about your age ... I warned you about this.'

'I understand.'

'Yes.' Patterson speared an oyster and conveyed it to his mouth. 'But this problem can be solved if you are willing to go along.'

She ate an oyster before asking, 'What does that mean?'

Patterson leaned towards her, looking directly at her, his

warm smile enveloping her.

'Has anyone told you how attractive you are?'

She stared down at the empty oyster shell, then looked up, meeting his gaze, her smoky blue eyes remote.

'Yes ... Dr Fosdick among others.'

Patterson freed another oyster from its shell.

'Yes ... I had forgotten Dr Fosdick. Well, the old lady is half blind, but not all that blind. I suggest when you see her tomorrow you should make yourself less attractive.'

'Am I to see her tomorrow?'

'At eleven o'clock, and please be punctual. She has a thing about time.'

They ate in silence. Patterson kept glancing at her. He could tell nothing from her calm expression of what was going on in her mind. The oysters finished, the waiter came to remove the plates. Patterson was growing uneasy. Could she be frigid? He didn't believe this: not with this sensuality that oozed out of her. She couldn't be, and yet she wasn't reacting to his charm. He felt that. She was cool, undisturbed by his smile. His smile had gained him so many easy conquests in the past. He moved restlessly as the waiter served the fish pie.

When he had gone, they ate for a moment in silence, then she said, 'This really is delicious.'

'I'm glad you like it.' He moved a morsel of pastry with his fork. 'I've told her about you. The fact you are Henry Oldhill's daughter made a big hit with her as I knew it must. But once the enthusiasm was over, she said: "She must be quite a child." I told her you were thirty-eight, serious, and I told her about your bowing arm. Then she said, "Why should a girl like that want to look after an old woman like me?" I got a bit of an inspiration.' Patterson sat back, smiling. He looked very pleased with himself. 'I told her you had always admired her playing, that you thought she was even greater than Myra Hess, and you would consider it a privilege to be of help.'

'Then you were telling the truth,' Sheila said quietly. 'It would be a privilege for me to do something for her and to hear her play again.'

Patterson cut into a lobster tail. He was becoming baffled by this woman. Was she serious or was she conning him? Didn't she realize that this whole operation was to be repaid by her getting into his bed? Or did she really imagine that a busy bank executive like himself would go to all this trouble, buy her an expensive dinner and then expect nothing in return except a polite thanks?

'Yes.' He ate for a moment, then decided to sink in a barb. 'She liked that of course. So she wants to see you. She did ask if I had found an alternative, and I have, just in case she still thinks, after she has met you, that you are too young.' He glanced to see her reaction, but her face remained calm and she seemed to be enjoying the fish pie as if he hadn't made the half-concealed threat. 'You see, Miss Oldhill, this is a little tricky for me. I mustn't lose Mrs Morely-Johnson's confidence. That's important to me and to the bank. I had to get another candidate lined up. In some ways, she is more suitable than you. She has had a lot of experience and she is around fifty-five. Mrs Morely-Johnson will be seeing her at ten o'clock tomorrow; you at eleven. Then she will make her decision.'

Sheila nodded.

'Of course,' she said in that quiet, controlled voice that always infuriated Hammett. 'I understand.'

They finished the fish pie and Patterson touched a bell to call the waiter.

'They have some marvellous desserts here. There's a strawberry sorbet . . .'

'I'd rather have just coffee, please.'

'Me too.' He told the waiter as he cleared the table to bring coffee, then he took out his heavy gold cigarette case, another gift from Mrs Morely-Johnson and offered it. When they had lit up and when the coffee had been served and the waiter gone, she said, 'Could you suggest, Mr Patterson, how I'm to make myself less attractive as you call it?'

He studied her.

'Alter your hair style. Make it more severe. No make up. Wear something dark. Lower your hem line and wear flat-heel shoes.'

She looked startled.

'You are quite an expert. I'll follow your suggestions.'

He took from his breast pocket a pair of spectacles, severe, oblong-shaped frames and put them on the table.

'I'd like you to wear these,' he went on. 'I got them after I talked to Mrs Morely-Johnson. They're plain glass. You won't need to wear them all the time, of course, but just put them on when you see her. They'll alter your appearance a lot.'

The waiter came with the coffee. When he had gone, she put the spectacles on, left her chair and looked at herself in the wall mirror. She returned to the table.

'You are quite right, Mr Patterson ... how clever of you, and thank you. You couldn't have been more helpful.'

Patterson pressed the dimple in his chin with his forefinger.

'I just want you to get the job. Look, I'm willing to bet you will get the job so we'll be seeing quite a lot of each other in the future. Could we drop the Mr Patterson–Miss Oldhill routine? My name's Chris, Sheila.'

'Of course.' She suddenly smiled. It was the first real smile he had had from her and in spite of the spectacles it made her even more attractive to him.

'For God's sake, take those glasses off ... they make you look like a school-marm.'

She laughed and removed the glasses.

'Better?' She pushed the sugar bowl towards him. 'I don't take it.'

'Nor do I. Well, that's settled then. You go to the Plaza Beach Hotel at eleven tomorrow morning. Ask the reception clerk for Mrs Morely-Johnson and tell him your name. I've already alerted him. There'll be no fuss.'

'How very efficient you are, Chris.'

'You could say that.' Patterson leaned back and smiled. He looked very sure and pleased with himself. 'Oh, there's your salary. I pay it from petty cash I handle for the old lady. I pay all her bills. The last one got a hundred a week ... everything found of course. You'll live in the penthouse. Your room is nice ... really lux ... TV ... everything. I suggested she should pay you a hundred and forty. She agreed. Okay?'

'Thank you. It's most generous.'

He had hoped for more than this. After all a hundred and forty with all found was damn good money, but she didn't react. He had had quite a tussle with the old lady to get her to agree.

They finished their coffee. There was a slight pause, then Sheila turned and looked pointedly at the red plush settee. Patterson followed the direction of her eyes.

'That interest you?' he said, trying to sound casual.

'I was just thinking it was convenient.' She looked at him and her eyes were again remote. 'Also the bolt on the door.'

He felt his heartbeat quicken.

'The bolt's unnecessary.' He was aware his voice was unsteady. 'After coffee is served the staff never intrude.'

She regarded him. The probing stare made him feel uncomfortable.

'You know that from experience?'

His warm smile now was a little forced.

'You could say that.'

'Chris...' She paused as she crushed out her cigarette, then she looked up and her lips moved into a half smile. 'I believe in paying my debts, but not this way.'

'Way? Sheila!' He pretended to be shocked. 'This means nothing ... there are no strings ... I wouldn't want you ...'

'Please!' She held up her hand. 'I take sex seriously. I think it is the most God-given experience and that it should never be abused. Sex to me is not taking off my pants and pulling my dress up to my neck and lying on a plush settee in an expensive restaurant where waiters don't intrude after the coffee has been served. But I always pay my debts. Could we talk about this when I have the job?'

For the first time since he could remember Patterson felt embarrassed. He also knew he was flushing and sweat beads had broken out on his forehead. He had never believed it would be an easy conquest, but this veiled promise of a future payment left him breathless.

'You don't have to talk like that,' he said unsteadily. 'I don't want you to get the wrong idea...'

She pushed back her chair.

'I will telephone you as soon as I know.'

He looked up at her as she got to her feet.

'Do you want to go?' He began to feel bewildered by the way she was controlling not only the conversation but now, the evening.

'I have to. I have letters to write before I go to bed and it is getting late.'

He knew now this was no ordinary woman and that his charm was a blunted weapon. But he wanted her as he had never wanted any other woman. He was shrewd enough to know that he had to give her free rein. *I pay my debts.*

Patience, he told himself.

'That's all right.' He got up and followed her to the door. While he was signing the check, she went down to the street.

He joined her.

'I can't thank you enough, Chris,' she said. 'I've enjoyed it so much and thank you again for ...'

'Let's hope it will work out,' he said. He was still thinking of what she had said. *I take sex seriously. I think it is a God-given experience* ... The thought of having her in his bed made him incoherent.

The doorman brought the Wildcat to the kerb. They drove in silence back to the Franklin Hotel. As Patterson pulled up, Sheila leaned towards him and brushed his cheek with her lips. Before he could reach for her, she was out of the car.

'Good night, Chris ... and again thanks.'

She ran up the steps and into the hotel lobby where Hammett was impatiently waiting.

Two

The following morning, Patterson arrived at his office at his usual time. He pulled a long face when he saw the pile of mail, arranged in two neat piles on his desk.

He had spent a restless night thinking about Sheila. She was certainly outspoken! *Sex to me isn't taking off my pants and pulling my dress up to my neck.* No other woman he had known ever talked that way and it had shaken him. But this bluntness was, in a way, encouraging. No inexperienced woman would have said a thing like that. He was also uneasy that she had so quickly realized the way his mind was working. Obviously she knew he had the hots for her and this irritated him. Had he been so blatant? And another thing: she had been in control all the time, and this he wasn't used to. This also irritated him. She was so goddamn calm. His charm had bounced off her. This had never happened before. *But I pay my debts.* That must mean, in her own time, when she was ready, she was prepared to go to bed with him ... what else could it mean?

He sat down at his desk and lit a cigarette.

Most of the night, and while he was showering and shaving, he had asked himself again and again just why this woman had set him on fire. It wasn't that she was beautiful, nor even pretty! He couldn't understand it. Yet he was obsessed with her: the thought of having her lying naked by his side in bed made him sick with desire. This urgency was something that hadn't happened to him before. He had lusted after many

23

women, but not in this gut-tearing, obsessive way. There was something extra in her that sparked this violent desire that half frightened, half elated him. What was it? Damn it! What was it?

Vera Cross, his secretary, came in. She was a pretty, neatly dressed girl in her late twenties and extremely efficient. The sight of her bouncing breasts and slim legs always helped Patterson through the daily grind of the day's routine. He had often wondered what she would be like in bed. This was something he wondered about when he looked at any attractive woman. He had an idea that she could be wildly enthusiastic, but he never went further than wondering. He was careful never to make a pass, although he was sure she wouldn't have objected if he had squeezed her bottom from time to time. But he had heard about one or two of his colleagues who had had it off with their secretaries and the trouble they had run into. He was ambitious. One day he hoped to be Vice-President – even President – of the bank. He knew one false move like that would finish him so he and Vera were good friends and it was strictly no hands.

'Good morning, Chris. The mail's heavy this morning,' Vera said, shutting the door. 'I've sorted the men from the boys. The right-hand pile is urgent.' She sat down, crossed one shapely leg over the other and flicked open her notebook.

With a suppressed groan, Patterson picked up the first letter. Driving himself, he disposed of the mail by 09.50. From time to time, as he read a letter, smoky blue eyes floated on the page, but he forced himself to concentrate. At 10.00, he had to attend the morning Board meeting which would last until 10.45.

'Any appointments, Vera?' he asked without hope.

'Every twenty minutes until lunch-time,' she said cheerfully. 'Mr Cohen is coming in at eleven. I've allotted him half an hour.'

Patterson clapped his hand to his forehead.

'But I haven't had time to look at his portfolio,' he said in dismay, remembering the previous afternoon, he had only thought of Sheila.

'I guessed that,' Vera said. 'I took it to Security. They've made suggestions. I told them you were too busy to cope.' She handed him two sheets of paper.

'I don't know what I'd do without you,' Patterson said and meant it. 'Thanks a million.'

Vera smiled happily.

'I knew you were tied up with these women for Mrs Morely-Johnson. Did you find anyone suitable?'

'I think so ... I'll know some time today. Thanks again, Vera,' and Patterson began to study the suggestions made by the Security department.

During the Board meeting which was pure routine, Patterson kept looking at his watch. By now Mrs Morely-Johnson would be talking to Mrs Fleming. The thought worried him. Suppose the old lady fell for this comfortable, elderly woman with fifteen years experience of being a companion? He had played her down, but with caution, pointing out that her educational background and her lack of musical knowledge might eventually become a bore. It had been gentle poison, but he thought it had made an impression on the old lady.

As he sat in his office, discussing with Bernie Cohen whether to shift half Cohen's holdings into short-term, high-yielding bonds, he kept looking at his desk clock. The time was now 11.10. Sheila would be sitting in the big, luxuriously furnished living-room of the penthouse suite, talking to the old lady. He felt his hands grow clammy. Suppose this flopped. What would Sheila do? She had said she was on her way to Los Angeles. Would she disappear from his life? The thought dismayed him.

Finally, he got rid of Bernie Cohen and then got involved with Mrs Van Davis who had surplus cash to invest. It was 11.40 before he got rid of her and as he conducted her to the lobby, he saw Vera signalling to him. Leaving Mrs Van Davis enveloped in his charm and warmth, he crossed quickly to Vera's desk.

'I have Mrs Morely-Johnson on the line.'

'Put her through,' he said and almost ran to his office. He shut the door, paused long enough to light a cigarette with unsteady fingers, then snatched up the telephone receiver.

'Is that you, Chris?' Mrs Morely-Johnson had a twanging accent, and when using the telephone, she had a rooted idea that everyone she spoke to was deaf. The first blast of her voice always made Patterson wince. He held the receiver away from his ear as he said, 'Good morning, Mrs Morely-Johnson. How are you this morning?'

'I'm all right. Maybe I'm feeling a little tired.' She liked to emphasize she was no longer young. 'It's about this girl ... Sheila Oldhill. I've talked to her. She seems a serious person, Chris.'

Patterson shifted in his chair. Careful to keep his voice

casual, he said, 'I think she is. She has excellent references. I've thoroughly investigated her (a lie). Did you like her?'

'Very much.' There was a pause, then the squawking voice went on. 'But she is very young.'

Patterson gripped the receiver, his nails turning white.

'Yes ... there is that. I hesitated whether to send her to you ... her qualifications...'

'I liked the other woman. This girl wouldn't have her experience.'

It's going to flop! Patterson thought.

'I understand perfectly, Mrs Morely-Johnson. Should I tell Miss Oldhill to look elsewhere?'

'I didn't say that!' Her voice rose a note and Patterson hurriedly shifted the receiver further from his ear. 'Not at all. The girl interests me. I knew her father ... he was a fine musician. It's a shame she knows so little about him. She tells me he was disappointed not to have a son. She tells me he ignored her... men can be so stupid. I would like to tell her more about her father. You are too young to remember. I often played when he was the leader of the orchestra.'

Patterson began to relax.

'I am sure she would be most grateful, Mrs Morely-Johnson.'

'I don't know about being grateful. A girl should know about her father. I've decided to take her on trial.'

Patterson rubbed the side of his jaw, aware he was sweating slightly.

'How about Mrs Fleming? Should I tell her to stand by?'

'Certainly not ... tell her I am suited. I will have this girl for three months. I've told her so. Then if I want to change, I'll consult you.'

Patterson drew in a long, slow breath, then said, 'I think you're being most wise. A three-month trial will tell you if she is what you are looking for.'

'Yes ... I thought that. And thank you very much, Chris, for being so helpful. I am sure it has taken up a lot of your time.'

'It is my pleasure.' Patterson put charm into his voice. 'Well, then that's settled for the moment. I have some transfers for you to sign. May I come about eleven tomorrow?'

'Of course.' There followed a girlish giggle that Patterson found gruesome. He had looked after her account now for the past four years and this old lady's adoration for him was hard to stomach. Okay, he had often told himself, she's old, a little dotty, lonely and she looks on me the way some old dears look on movie stars. She's harmless, but I wish to God she wouldn't try to be so goddamn girlish!

'Fine, Mrs Morely-Johnson. When is Miss Oldhill starting with you?'

'She's moving in right away.'

Patterson frowned. This wasn't good news. Once Sheila was with the old lady, access to her – intimate access – could be difficult.

'Do you want me to pay her weekly or monthly?' he asked.

'The girl hasn't any money. Her father left her nothing. She tells me he left his money to a home for old musicians. I am really surprised ... but musicians can be eccentric. I admit it ... sometimes I'm eccentric.' Again the girlish giggle that set Patterson's teeth on edge. 'I've decided I will pay her. I have given her some money to buy clothes. She is rather shabbily dressed. You know how snobby people are in this hotel. She is now out buying some clothes. I won't worry you with her affairs, Chris. You have enough to do without that.'

Patterson's eyes narrowed as he listened. Sheila had certainly worked fast, he thought. Suddenly, she was out of his control. He was sure she had talked the old lady into this new arrangement. For the past four years he had always paid the wages of the old lady's companion.

'It would have been no problem.' He had to force his voice to sound casual. 'Well then, I look forward to seeing you to-morrow morning, Mrs Morely-Johnson. Is there anything I can bring you?'

'That reminds me. I was going to ask.' A long pause, then she went on, 'Will you please bring me five thousand dollars in cash?'

Patterson could scarcely believe what she was saying. He leaned forward, his elbows resting on his desk, his fingers tightly gripping the receiver.

'Did you say five thousand, Mrs Morely-Johnson?'

'Yes, please. I think I should have more cash here. I don't always like paying by cheque.'

'I will happily bring it.'

He listened to more of Mrs Morely-Johnson's yak and when she finally hung up, he stared thoughtfully at his blotter.

He didn't like this new development. He felt he had been, suddenly and unexpectedly, deprived of some of his power. Had Sheila, in some clever way, persuaded the old lady to pay her and not to be paid by the bank? Maybe he was imagining this whereas the old lady had thought this up for herself. *She is out buying clothes.* Had this really been the old lady's idea or had Sheila suggested it? He pressed his forefinger against his dimple as he thought. And now the old lady was asking for five thousand dollars in cash! This again made him feel uneasy. She had never asked for cash before. Thinking about the past, he realized how complete his control had been over her during the past four years. He had paid her tax, invested her money; every item she bought he had paid for: her hotel bills, her chauffeur's wages, the car repairs, her gifts to charities and up to now, her companion's wages and expenses had passed through his hands.

I've decided to pay her myself. I won't worry you with her affairs.

He didn't like this sudden change. He wondered if the old lady had been persuaded.

He lit a cigarette as he thought. He saw the calm, expressionless face, the smoky blue eyes, the firm mouth. Then he heard her quiet voice as she said: *I pay my debts.* He began to relax. He told himself that he was imagining something that didn't exist. The old lady was a little eccentric. What did it matter if she paid Sheila herself? What was he worrying about? The important thing now was, sooner or later, Sheila would pay her debt.

Vera put her head around his door.

'Mr Lessing is waiting.'

Patterson stubbed out his cigarette.

'Send him in, Vera,' he said and with an effort he switched his mind off his immediate problems and reached for a scratch pad and his gold pencil.

Jack Bromhead had been Mrs Morely-Johnson's chauffeur for the past five years. Although Mrs Morely-Johnson was in awe of him, she was very proud to have such a man as her chauffeur. Aged fifty-five, Bromhead was tall, lean and dignified and his thick hair was the colour of burnished silver. Once, when sightseeing in Canterbury, England, Mrs Morely-Johnson had seen a Bishop walking along the main street. His benign expression, his dignity, his snow white hair had made an impression on her. She had the same impression when Bromhead had come to her from an Agency to apply for the vacancy caused by the death of her previous chauffeur who had been far from dignified, too familiar and who thought a Cadillac the only car in the world.

Bromhead had impeccable references. He had only recently arrived in America, being British born. He had told her he had been chauffeur to the Duke of Sussex. His quiet, dignified manners, his references from the Duke, his appearance made him irresistible to Mrs Morely-Johnson.

He told her in his quiet, beautifully modulated voice that he was used to driving only a Rolls-Royce. If Mrs Morely-Johnson preferred the Cadillac, and here he paused, lifting his silver grey eyebrows, then he would regretfully have to look elsewhere.

Looking at this tall, stately man, Mrs Morely-Johnson thought how her friends would envy her having such a personality working for her. She had never thought of buying a Rolls-Royce. All her friends had either Cadillacs or Mercedes. The idea delighted her. She told him to get a Rolls. He had inclined his head gravely and she was a shade disappointed that he wasn't more pleased. He then told her that he would prefer to get his uniforms from Hawes & Curtis, London, who were the Duke of Edinburgh's tailors. He thought American tailors didn't have the style to which he was accustomed. Slightly bewildered, but enchanted, Mrs Morely-Johnson told him to go ahead and make the necessary arrangements. Even when the check came in for over a thousand dollars, she paid it without flinching. She assured herself that so dignified and handsome a man had to be suitably dressed.

It was only when the gleaming plum coloured Rolls-Royce arrived at the entrance of the Plaza Beach Hotel plus Bromhead in an immaculate grey uniform with black piping, plus a cockade in his peaked cap that she realized she was getting value for money. The doorman of the hotel who had seen everything and appeared to be unimpressionable, was impressed, and that alone made Mrs Morely-Johnson's day.

On the first of every December, Bromhead had suggested politely but with steely firmness that she should trade in the Rolls for the new model. Every year, Mrs Morely-Johnson happily agreed.

Mrs Morely-Johnson had engaged Bromhead a year before Chris Patterson had taken over her affairs and this had been fortunate for Bromhead. Had Patterson engaged him, he would have investigated his references and he would have found there was no such person as the Duke of Sussex, and the elaborate crest as well as the reference, written in a spidery hand, were forgeries.

Jack Bromhead had spent ten years of his fifty-five years in prison for forgery. He was recognized by the British police as one of the most expert forgers in the country. He could not only forge any signature, but he was also expert in reproducing any document or currency notes, being a top-class engraver.

Having spent a bleak ten years in prison due to a tip-off by a dissatisfied partner, Bromhead had decided that forgery was now too dangerous a career to pursue. At his age, he felt he wanted a calmer life, but a life with prospects. Released from prison, he decided to capitalize on his appearance by going to America. He was an expert driver and he felt with his English accent, his looks and his dignity, he couldn't fail to make an impact on some rich American.

He arrived on the Pacific coast with enough money to last him for several weeks – money he had obtained by selling his stock of engraving plates to another of his colleagues who was willing to take any risk, and presented himself at the leading domestic agency.

He knew exactly what he wanted: to be a chauffeur to a rich, elderly woman and he was fortunate that Mrs Morely-Johnson had that morning asked the Agency to find her a chauffeur.

During his years as a master forger, Bromhead had enjoyed an income of thirty thousand pounds sterling a year, but those heydays only lasted for less than three years before the police had caught up with him. But during that time, he had acquired the taste for luxury and the ten bleak years in prison had badly shaken him. When he had been released, he told himself that he must find a police-free method of taking care of his old age. He knew he would never be able to face another ten years in jail.

His thinking was thus: Give me a rich old woman, give me time, and if I don't fix it so I live in comfort for the rest of my days, then I don't deserve anything.

He was acutely aware that if he made one false move and gave the police any reason to investigate his past he would be in serious trouble. He was fifty-five years of age: there was time. As Mrs Morely-Johnson's chauffeur he led a comfortable, easy life. He had a good room with a shower and television, in a small block of apartments reserved for the chauffeurs of the rich Plaza Beach Hotel's clients. Being the chauffeur of the only Rolls-Royce gave him a status symbol with the other chauffeurs which pleased him. He was paid one hundred dollars a week with everything found. Mrs Morely-Johnson wasn't exacting. Each morning at 11.00, she went shopping and Bromhead drove her, took her parcels and generally acted as a nursemaid, but this didn't worry him. She seldom wanted to be taken for drives in the afternoon and she never went out at night. She preferred to play the piano or to give lunch and dinner parties on her terrace and the hotel staff took care of that. She also liked to sit in the sun, listening to her hi-fi set playing gramophone discs.

Bromhead had plenty of time. He spent some of this time writing to movie stars, authors and other celebrities asking for their autographs. Such is the delight of such people to be asked for their autographs, he received a steady supply and to keep his forging hand in, he perfected their signatures so that he could produce them without hesitation on any blank cheque should the need arise. But this, of course, was dangerous. Forging these signatures was purely an exercise and not to be capitalized.

When he had arrived for the first time at the Plaza Beach Hotel he knew nothing about Mrs Morely-Johnson except that she was wealthy. How wealthy he didn't know, but he was determined to find out. He invested in a highly sophisticated bugging device, the microphones of which he planted in Mrs Morely-Johnson's living-room, on the terrace and in her bedroom. These microphones, little bigger than grape seeds, were powerful enough to feed a tape recorder in Bromhead's room across the courtyard.

He had accepted the fact that this was to be a long-term operation and was prepared to be patient. A year passed without him gaining any information of value, except that he learned Mrs Morely-Johnson was inclined to gush over men much, much younger than herself. It wasn't until Chris Patterson appeared on the scene that the information that Bromhead wanted began to filter through on the tape.

Sitting in his comfortable room, listening to Patterson's voice on his first visit to the penthouse, at long last, he heard details of Mrs Morely-Johnson's financial affairs. He had a scratch pad on his knee and he made rapid notes. He learned that apart from her jewellery, her Rolls, her furs, her pictures and her real-estate investments, she was worth around five million dollars. Looking at his notes when the interview was over, Bromhead realized if he played the right cards, he had found Eldorado.

Another year went by. The routine was always the same, but this suited Bromhead. Gradually, he increased his hold on the old lady. Nothing was too much trouble. Her every whim was dealt with with quiet, kindly dignity which delighted her. Bromhead was looking to the future. But during these passing months he became more and more aware that Patterson was making a much bigger impact on the old lady than he was. He was prepared for this. He now knew she was susceptible to the young and the handsome. He had often noticed her reaction to young men who served her in the luxury stores and how she sat on her terrace, before the cataract had made her half blind, with powerful field-glasses, watching young men parade along the waterfront. So it came as no surprise that Patterson, remarkably handsome, young and well dressed, was giving the old lady a jolt like a massive shot of hormones.

Then one morning, she told Bromhead to go to her attorney's office.

'I want you to bring Mr Weidman back here, Bromhead,' she said, 'and when we have finished our business talk to take him back to his office. He will like a little ride in the Rolls.'

'Certainly, ma'am,' Bromhead had said.

Business talk . . .

Before collecting Mr Weidman, Bromhead arranged a large spool of tape on his recorder, set the time switch to begin recording at 11.00 when Mr Weidman was due to arrive.

He sat in the Rolls outside the hotel, knowing every word between Mrs Morely-Johnson and her attorney would be recorded while he waited for the attorney to reappear. He drove him back to his office. Then returning to his own room, he made himself a ham sandwich, opened a can of beer and settled down to listen to the play-back.

Mrs Morely-Johnson was leaving two million dollars to the Cancer Research Fund. Two million dollars, plus 1,000 acres of building land to Oxfam. A million dollars to the blind. Her pictures were to be sold and the proceeds (perhaps two million dollars) to UNICEF.

Then followed the bequests:

An annuity of $100,000 to be paid to Christopher Patterson for his life time in recognition for his constant kindness and attention. An annuity of $15,000 to Jack Bromhead and the Rolls-Royce. An annuity of $20,000 to Miss May Lawson, her companion-help.

There had been a pause of silence on the tape, then her attorney's voice asked, 'How about your nephew, Gerald Hammett? Are you providing for him?'

'Gerald?' Mrs Morely-Johnson's voice shot up. 'Certainly not! He's a horrible boy! He will get nothing from me!'

There was a lot more, but it wasn't important. Bromhead sat

back and studied his notes.

An annuity of $15,000, plus the Rolls-Royce wasn't what he expected. This must be readjusted ... somehow. At the moment he didn't know how.

Her nephew, Gerald Hammett? Who was he? This was the first time that Bromhead knew that Mrs Morely-Johnson had a relative.

After some thought, he cleaned the tape and locked his notes away. There was time, he told himself. The nephew interested him. He now needed to make inquiries. A relative could upset a will ... wills were tricky, and he had to be careful. One false move and the police would arrive. He flinched at the thought.

Then he remembered Solly Marks. Before he had been re-leased from prison, he had been told by the man who shared his cell that if ever he needed anything when on the Pacific coast, the man to contact was Solly Marks. This man lived in Los Angeles, some hundred miles from where Bromhead was now living. Solly Marks was a shyster lawyer, a property owner, a money-lender and a man with his ear to the ground.

After some thought, Bromhead decided he had to have help and Solly Marks, seemed, on recommendation, to be the man to help him. He found his telephone number and called him. As soon as Bromhead had mentioned the name of the man with whom he had shared his cell and mentioned his own name, Marks had become exttemely co-operative.

'I'll come over,' he said. 'Better not talk on the phone. You name the place and I'll be there.'

'Book in at the Franklin Hotel,' Bromhead said. 'I'll meet you there at six o'clock tomorrow evening.'

Bromhead had a slight shock when he saw Marks sitting in the lounge of the hotel, waiting for him. The man looked like an inflated toad: short, squat with tremendously wide shoulders, his face resembling a ping-pong ball with tufts of reddish hair glued to its sides. His features disappeared into fat. His small, black eyes, peering out from puffy bastions were like jet beads, sparkling, lively, cunning and shrewd.

Yet within minutes of talking, Bromhead knew this was the man he was looking for.

'You don't have to know why,' he said as they began to talk business. 'This is what I want: I want a complete breakdown on Mrs Morely-Johnson who lives at the Plaza Beach Hotel. I want the same on Christopher Patterson, the assistant manager of the Pacific Traders Bank. When I say a breakdown, I want all details about him: especially about his sex life. Then I want details of Gerald Hammett, Mrs Morely-Johnson's nephew. Can you do this?'

Marks laid a small hand that looked like a lump of badly fashioned dough on Bromhead's arm.

'I can do anything, but at a price. I don't imagine you could pay just yet, but would you say you have good prospects?'

Bromhead stared into the tiny, black eyes.

'I have good prospects.'

Marks finished his drink.

'Then there is no problem. I will get the information for you. Could I ask what are your prospects?'

Bromhead allowed his stern features to relax in a smile.

'I collect autographs,' he said. 'It is a little childish, but I have my reasons.' He took from his pocket a scratch pad and offered it to Marks. 'Would you mind giving me yours?'

Marks stared at him, then his tiny mouth like a knife cut in a lump of dough moved slightly into what might be mistaken for a smile. He took the pad, produced a pen and scrawled his signature: a shapeless mess of squiggles.

Bromhead studied the signature for several minutes.

'Not easy,' he said under his breath, then he turned the sheet on to a fresh page, borrowed Marks's pen and reproduced the signature. He tore off the two sheets from the pad, shuffled them and handed them to Marks.

'Which is the one you wrote?' he asked.

Marks looked at the two identical signatures, tore the sheets into little pieces and nodded at Bromhead.

'Impressive,' he said. 'Very well, my friend, you have un-limited credit.'

'Fair enough,' Bromhead said. 'What will it cost me?'

'Ten thousand dollars for the research.'

Bromhead shook his head.

'No ... five thousand. It's only worth five thousand.'

Marks leaned forward. He looked like an over-fed vulture.

'Mrs Morely-Johnson is worth five million dollars. Never cut corners, my friend ... ten thousand or we don't do a deal.'

'Eight,' Bromhead said without any hope.

Marks gave a shrill little laugh.

'I said ten ... I'll be in touch with you,' and climbing to his feet, he waddled away towards the elevator.

Bromhead watched him go. This was a man after his own heart.

The dossier that Marks finally delivered was exactly what Bromhead required.

Before parting with the dossier, Marks had asked for an I.O.U. for $10,000, and this Bromhead had given him. He was so certain his plan would eventually succeed that he was confident that sooner or later he would be in the position to repay Marks. Even the 25 per cent interest charged by Marks didn't make him hesitate for more than a second or so before he signed.

'If there's anything else I can do for you,' Marks said, putting the I.O.U. away carefully in his billfold, 'you know how to contact me. It will be my pleasure.'

At this rate of interest, Bromhead thought, this was an understatement, but he had what he wanted and he had long ago learned that if you wanted something important you had to expect to pay for it.

He settled down to study the dossier, beginning with the information concerning Gerald Hammett who he considered a danger spot being the only likely contestant of Mrs Morely-Johnson's will.

He learned that Gerald was the only child of Lawson Hammett, Mrs Morely-Johnson's brother, a reasonably successful mining engineer who had been killed in a mining accident some eight years ago. His wife had run off with Hammett's best friend and he had obtained a divorce with the custody of the child, Gerald. Father and son hadn't got along together. In spite of making efforts, Lawson Hammett found he had no point of contact with the boy who was lazy, dirty and had a vicious temper. When Gerald left school, instead of returning home, he disappeared. His father, relieved, had made no effort to find him.

On his twenty-second birthday, Gerald who by now had learned that if you don't ask, you don't get, called on his aunt, Mrs Morely-Johnson at the Plaza Beach Hotel and he reminded her in no uncertain terms that he was her nephew and what was she going to do for him?

Had he approached the old lady with tact and politeness she would have done something for him, but he had no time for rich old women and he demanded financial aid in a way that shocked his aunt.

Marks's investigator had talked to an eye-witness of the meeting. The doorman of the Plaza Beach Hotel remembered the incident, now five years ago and was prepared to describe it in detail for a $10 bill. Gerald had arrived at the hotel, dirty, shabby and bearded just as Mrs Morely-Johnson was going out for her morning shopping. As the result of smoking a reefer to bolster his courage, Gerald was in an ugly and truculent mood. He had confronted his aunt in the hotel lobby and told her in a loud voice what he expected of her. The old lady listened to this dirty-looking boy, scarcely able to believe her ears. She was aware that her so-called friends were also listening and staring. She felt helpless and she looked at the doorman who hadn't seen Gerald's entrance, waving her hands in a signal of distress.

The doorman, remembering many past favours, grabbed hold of Gerald and ejected him from the hotel with considerable violence but not before Gerald had yelled, 'Okay, you stupid old cow ... if you don't want me, then up yours!'

It had been a scene that took Mrs Morely-Johnson some time to live down. Had she not been worth five million dollars, the manager of this luxury hotel would have asked her to leave.

According to the dossier, Gerald had then gone to Los Angeles. He had joined up with a Hippy group and had spent the next three years living rough, scratching up some kind of living until he finally opted to become a drug pusher. This enterprise lasted less than two months before the Vice squad caught up with him. His father now dead, he had only Mrs Morely-Johnson to turn to. A detective called on her and asked her if she was prepared to do anything for her nephew. The detective happened to be a handsome Negro. Mrs Morely-Johnson had been born and raised in Georgia and couldn't bear the sight of a black skin. Apart from loathing her nephew who had practically wrecked her way of living at the Plaza Beach Hotel, talking to a black detective was, to her, the uttermost end. She dismissed him with a wave of her hand.

Gerald spent two years behind bars. During that time he brooded and finally came to the conclusion that he had been badly treated from childhood, that the world owed him a living and Mrs Morely-Johnson should be made to pay. This was, of course, a deduction offered by Marks's investigator and Bromhead was prepared to go along with it. In Gerald's place, he would have felt the same way. When he was released, Gerald had gone to New York and to the Hippy scene, but he left drugs alone. He knew he was now a marked man and if the police had reason to arrest him again, he would go away for a long time.

It was during this time when he was living in a vacuum that he met Veda Rayson. She was young, pretty and willing, and what was more important, she had a comfortable income from her father who was thankful not to have her living in his house. Gerald and she teamed up and she let him live with her in her two-room apartment, paid the bills and generally made his life comfortable. The four months he lived with her turned Gerald soft. He came to like this way of life. He hadn't to get out of bed before eleven o'clock in the morning. He had his meals provided. When he needed clothes, he had only to ask. Also, Veda happened to be the most exciting lay he had had so far. So what could you want better, man? he asked himself.

Then one morning as Gerald, waking, was turning Veda on her back, she gave a tiny, suppressed scream that frightened him. Then followed the commotion of telephoning, getting an ambulance, having her dragged down the spiral staircase in a hammock by two boozy-faced ambulance men with Gerald, shaking and panic in his heart, following them and offering useless advice.

At the hospital the nurse had told him there was no hope. Marks's investigator hadn't wasted time going into details but it seemed Veda had been fighting cancer for the past year. The investigator had picked up gossip from the hospital receptionist. The nurse who had broken the news to Gerald had been Sheila Oldhill, and the receptionist said that this woman had no right to be a nurse.

'She is a Tom-cat,' the receptionist said. 'I know all about her. Show her any man and she'll fall flat on her back.'

The investigator sighed. If this was true then Sheila Oldhill was his dream woman, but he didn't say this to the receptionist.

Veda died within thirty-eight hours of being admitted to the hospital. Again it was Nurse Oldhill who had broken the news to Gerald who felt a pang of loss. Who was going to pay the rent, feed him, buy his clothes?

'I was watching them,' the receptionist told the investigator. 'It was horrible. She was looking hungrily at him ... that is the only word to describe it. How could she look at a dirty, hairy kid like that?'

The investigator, a fat, middle-aged man had seen everything and heard everything. What the receptionist told him was so much grist to his mill.

He investigated further and learned that Sheila Oldhill and Gerald had set up home together – a two-room apartment. Sheila continued to work at the hospital, providing the funds on which they lived. Gerald spent his days listening to pop music, going to movies and waiting for Sheila to return. At the conclusion of the report, they were still in New York: she was working at the hospital, he living on her.

All this interested Bromhead. Before making a decision, he telephoned Marks, asking him for a breakdown on Sheila Oldhill. This took a further two weeks and cost Bromhead another I.O.U. for two thousand dollars, but when he read the report he considered he was getting value for money.

He learned that Sheila's father had been first violinist with the New York Philharmonic Orchestra and referring to Mrs Morely-Johnson's dossier he learned at one time she had been a concert pianist – her professional name being Alice Lesson – and had played with the Philharmonic Orchestra a number of times.

It was only when he studied Chris Patterson's dossier and discovered how highly sexed he was and learned of the numerous affairs he was having out of town and the caution he used to prevent any gossip that Bromhead began to perfect his plan to take care of his future in comfort.

After more thought, he decided he must meet Gerald and Sheila Oldhill. There was now a sense of urgency because Mrs Morely-Johnson was without a companion-help. The old lady was waiting to hear from the doctors. Her companion who had been with her for fifteen years had been taken to hospital. Mrs Morely-Johnson disliked change and was prepared to wait for her companion to recover rather than to look elsewhere, but Bromhead was sure the companion wouldn't recover and he would have to act swiftly.

He wrote to Gerald on the Plaza Beach Hotel notepaper, stating he was coming to New York on urgent business and he would like Gerald to meet him at the Kennedy Airport. Then he asked Mrs Morely-Johnson if he could take the week-end off as his brother (non-existent) was arriving in New York and Mrs Morely-Johnson was happy not only for him to meet his brother but to give him his fare there and back.

Before leaving for New York, he contacted Solly Marks and told him he was in urgent need of $1,000. Marks sent him the money without hesitation for Marks now realized that Bromhead was planning something that could be big. Marks, like Bromhead, kept thinking of Mrs Morely-Johnson's five million dollars. Marks didn't want to know any details. He knew Bromhead was serious. When Bromhead made his kill, then Marks would move in, but not before. The police couldn't touch him so long as he acted only as a money-lender and this Marks was willing to do.

Bromhead was a little disappointed in Gerald Hammett, but he was philosophical enough to know that a good workman could use inferior tools if he had to. As soon as he had told Gerald he was Mrs Morely-Johnson's chauffeur, Gerald who had been eyeing him with suspicion became much more alive. Bromhead told him part of the plan, but gave no details. He then asked if Sheila Oldhill could be relied on to help.

Gerald said she could.

Bromhead then asked if he could meet her. As they drove in Gerald's Volkswagen, which Sheila had bought him, to the two-room apartment, Bromhead thought of the possibilities. If this woman was a Tom-cat, as the receptionist at the hospital had claimed, then she was the woman he wanted. Looking at Gerald as he drove, Bromhead decided this immature boy wouldn't fall for a non-sexy woman. A woman so much older than he, had to be right.

Bromhead was immediately impressed by Sheila. Although now, at his age, he no longer bothered with women, he was immediately aware of her sensuality, her calmness and her efficiency. With this woman, he told himself, he couldn't go wrong.

Having explained his plan, he warned them that until Mrs Morely-Johnson's companion either died or was proved unfit to resume her duties, the plan wasn't on. He was a little worried about Gerald who sat away from them, listening and scowling. Whenever he began to speak, Sheila had raised her hand, stopping him and he had muttered a four-letter word under his breath, then kept silent.

Bromhead looked directly at Sheila.

'What do you say?'

'It is worth a try,' she said quietly.

'This is a gamble,' Bromhead said. 'It may not come off. I want you both to think of it as a long-term operation, but the pay-off will be big.'

Gerald, across the room, chewed his thumb-nail.

'What do you call long-term for God's sake?'

Bromhead regarded him.

'We will have to wait until the old lady dies.' He paused, then went on, 'But no one lives for ever.'

Three

Gerald Hammett sat in his shabby room at the Franklin Hotel with the door ajar and waited anxiously for Sheila's return. She had left the hotel at 10.45 and he reckoned she would be back with news by at least 12.30. At 13.00 he went down to the bar and bought a beef sandwich and a glass of beer. From his stool in the bar he could see the entrance of the hotel. He was growing impatient and worried. At 13.30, he returned to his room and again waited. The hands of his watch crept on. What had happened to her? She was the king-pin of this operation and without her, there would be no more money. Had she been knocked down by a car? He was angry and frustrated to realize that although his own part in the plan was of vital importance, he had such a small active part to play.

Sheila and Bromhead were so goddamn efficient, he thought angrily. It seemed to him that they treated him the way movie stars would treat a bit player and this riled him.

Around 16.00 when almost exasperated with waiting, he saw her come down the corridor, carrying three boxes and several parcels that told him she had been on a shopping spree.

He waited until she had unlocked her door, then he came out into the corridor, looked right and left to assure himself there was no one to see him and then joined her as she entered her room.

'What happened for God's sake?' he demanded as she closed the door.

'You shouldn't be here, Gerry,' she said as she dropped the boxes on the bed. 'You're taking too many risks.'

Gerald said a four-letter word.

'What happened?'

'It's all right. I'm on a three months' trial.' She crossed to the fly-blown mirror and began to rearrange her hair which she had dressed low, making her look older and severe.

'What's all this?' Gerald demanded, waving to the boxes on the bed.

'Oh, clothes.' Her voice was indifferent. 'Your aunt wants me to dress better.'

'Did she give you the money?'

'Of course.'

He stared at the boxes.

'What's she paying you?'

'A hundred and forty a week.'

'She is?' Gerald whistled. 'That's not hay, man! The old cow must be rolling in the stuff.'

'We know that.'

Her cold tone made him stare at her.

'And Patterson?'

'I was able to persuade him.'

'Just what the hell does that mean?'

'Never mind. I must pack. She wants me there by six o'clock. I haven't much time.'

'You mean you are going to live with her right now?'

'Yes ... she is without anyone.'

Gerald shifted uneasily.

'What's going to happen to me?'

She moved by him, took a suitcase from the closet, put it on the bed and opened it.

He caught hold of her arm and swung her around to face him.

'Did you hear me? What's going to happen to me?'

She regarded him with her calm, smoky blue eyes and this quiet calmness angered and frightened him.

'You accepted the arrangement,' she said and jerked her arm free. 'Be careful ... you will bruise me.'

'I'll do more than that!' Gerald snarled and hooking his foot around her ankle, he upset her, sprawling her on her back across the boxes on the bed.

As he dropped on her, his hand groping for her skirt, she struck him across his face. Water jumped into his eyes and he felt blood starting from his nose. Stunned by the force of the blow, he felt her move out from under him, then a Kleenex tissue was thrust into his hand. He sat up, the tissue held to his nose while he glared at her.

'You bitch!'

'Control yourself,' she said curtly. 'Get off the bed ... you're bleeding.'

Trembling and now in despair, he got to his feet.

'I know the signs, you bitch,' he mumbled as he dabbed at his nose. 'You've got the hots for this banker bastard. I don't mean anything any more to you.'

'Stop talking,' she said. This quiet, firm voice made him feel like a performing ape who answers to signals. He sat on the sagging chair and she went into the bathroom, returning with a wet sponge. With expert and completely impersonal hands, she wiped the blood off his nose and mouth. Then she returned to the bathroom, rinsed out the sponge while he sat there like a beaten child.

'Gerry...' She stood in the bathroom doorway, looking at him. 'I haven't much time, but we must talk. This is a big operation. You have to agree to it. Bromhead knows his business. I know my business. We could be rich for life and this is what I want. You must stop behaving like an idiot child. You ask what is going to happen to you. You are important to this plan, but you have a waiting part. If you can't think what is going to happen to you, then I can make suggestions.'

Gerald dabbed at his nose with the blood-stained tissue.

'So what are your goddamn suggestions?'

'I will give you seventy dollars a week: that is half what I'm being paid,' Sheila said. 'You must leave here ... it's too expensive. You must find a cheap room. With seventy dollars a week you should be able to manage. You could even get a job.'

Gerald dropped the tissue on the floor. He sniffed, rubbing the back of his hand across his nose and then looked suspiciously to see if his hand was bloody.

'Job? What are you talking about? What the hell could I do?'

She regarded him.

'All right ... never mind. You must manage on seventy dollars a week ... a lot of people do.'

'And in the meantime this banker bastard will be screwing you?'

'Gerry ... will you please leave me? I have to pack. To-morrow, you leave here. This is the beginning of an operation that could change our lives. Will you please try to act like an adult?'

He glared at her.

'Suppose I don't want this money?' he said. 'Money can bring trouble. Get on that bed, baby, I want you.'

Still the calm expression, but the smoky blue eyes came alive.

'Get out!' There was a sudden snap in her voice that scared Gerald. 'I must pack!'

He got reluctantly to his feet.

'How am I to find a room?' There was now a whine in his voice. 'It's fine for you, living in luxury with that old cow and having it off with that banker bastard ... how do I find a room?'

'Gerald! Will you get out!' She looked around, caught up her handbag, opened it and tossed money on the bed. 'There . . . seventy dollars! You won't get any more until this day week!'

He looked at the bills lying on the bed, hesitated, then picked them up and shoved them into his hip-pocket.

'The trouble with you is you only think of money,' he said.

'Is that what you think? You have to have money to live. The trouble with you is you don't think of money – you rely on me to keep you.'

'We were happy as we were,' he said, moving to the door. 'I hate this goddamn thing you've got mixed up with.'

'Send me your new address at the Plaza Beach Hotel,' she said not looking at him. 'I'll call you.'

He stood by the door, hesitating, then he said, 'Come on, baby, before I go . . . drop your pants.'

She stared at him, calm and remote.

'Please go, Gerry . . . I have to pack.'

It was the coldness in her voice and the indifference in her smoky blue eyes that told him he could have lost her and he felt suddenly scared and insecure. Knowing it would be useless to try to persuade her when she was in this mood, he went out, slamming the door.

She listened as he stamped down the corridor. When his door slammed, she sat on the edge of the bed, surrounded by the boxes of clothes she had bought, and pressed her hands to her eyes.

Around 11.00 the following morning, Patterson parked the Wildcat outside the Plaza Beach Hotel. He walked up the impressive flight of marble steps that led to the hotel lobby.

The doorman saluted him. He was a big, red-faced man who had adapted himself to the whims of the rich old freaks – as he regarded them – who lived in the hotel.

'Morning, Mr Patterson.'

'Hi, Tom.' Patterson paused. He believed in being friendly with underlings. It cost him nothing and it paid dividends. 'How's the wife?'

The doorman grimaced.

'Like me, Mr Patterson . . . getting no younger.'

'Oh, nonsense. Talking about getting no younger, did you hear the one about . . .' and he recounted the raw story he had heard from a client just before leaving the bank. The doorman spluttered with laughter as Patterson entered the lobby.

As he crossed to the elevators, he ran into Herman Lacey, the Director of the hotel. Lacey was tall and thin with a balding head, white sideboards and a hawk-like face that made him look like a successful senator.

The two men shook hands.

'How's Mrs Morely-Johnson?' Patterson asked.

Lacey took a personal interest in all his clients. He lifted his elegant shoulders.

'Very blind now. I wish you would talk to her. An operation these days is so simple. Otherwise, I would say she is well. She seems pleased with her new companion. I would have thought a woman a little older ... but Mrs Morely-Johnson seems satisfied.' Again he shrugged his shoulders.

'I wish I could persuade her about the operation,' Patterson said in all sincerity. 'But that is a topic that doesn't go down well. As for Miss Oldhill ... I persuaded the old lady to take her. They are both musicians and I think it will give the old lady an extra interest.'

'I didn't know. Yes ... I see ... a musician? How interesting.'

The door of the elevator swung open. Patterson shook hands and leaving Lacey, he was whisked to the 20th floor of the hotel and to the penthouse.

As the elevator mounted, he again felt a rush of blood run through him at the thought of seeing Sheila again.

He had been disappointed and irritated that she hadn't contacted him. He had expected her to telephone him – he felt that was the least she could have done – to tell him that she had got the job which, after all, had been entirely due to his influence. He had had the news from Mrs Morely-Johnson, but Sheila – he was thinking of her now as Sheila – surely could have found time to have told him herself and to have thanked him.

Leaving the elevator, he crossed the small vestibule and pressed the bell push of the penthouse. As he stood waiting, he was aware that his heartbeat had accelerated and his hands had become clammy.

Sheila opened the door.

'Good morning, Mr Patterson ... please come in.'

He stood there, looking at her. He scarcely recognized this tall, severe-looking woman with her glasses, her hair dressed in an unbecoming style. She was wearing a white blouse with a high collar and a black skirt. She looked immaculate, efficient, sexless and remote.

As she stood aside, Patterson, a little dazed by this unexpected transformation, walked into the lobby.

'Is that you, Chris?' The raucous squawk came from the living-room: the door stood open.

Without looking at him, Sheila moved to the door.

'It's Mr Patterson,' she said and stood aside for Patterson to pass her. Again he tried to catch her eye, but she was already walking into the room that was used as her office and he had no alternative but to walk into the living-room.

Mrs Morely-Johnson was sitting in a lounging chair in this big, elegant room with its six windows looking out onto the terrace with its mass of flowers and that overlooked the Pacific ocean and the town.

Mrs Morely-Johnson was a bird-like woman with bright, alive blue eyes and a deeply tanned skin that was creased like old, well-worn leather. She made no attempt to conceal her age. She could have afforded the most expensive facial treatments but these she shunned. She was confident that her personality was so strong that she could ignore wrinkles and a leathery skin and yet still be attractive to young men. It wasn't her personality that attracted them – it was her money, but this she was vain enough not to believe. She loved diamonds and her beautiful long fingers carried many flashing rings. Her thin, wrinkled wrists carried platinum and diamond bracelets. The jewels she festooned herself with every morning were often worth more than $300,000. The cataract on her eyes had worsened, but she was still able to see, although print and handwriting now floated in an out-of-focus haze. This didn't worry her. She could still make out people's faces and with the aid of her powerful spectacles the beauty of the young male wasn't denied her.

She regarded Patterson, leaning forward and peering at him, as he came into the room. He was really the most attractive man she had known, she thought. His warmth, his handsomeness and his easy manner delighted her.

'Chris!' She extended her beautiful hand, flashing with diamonds. 'So you have come to worry me?'

The roguish note in her voice made Patterson's heart sink. She was in one of those moods.

'Just a few transfers,' he said, seating himself beside her, but not before he had brushed her hand with his lips: a gesture he knew pleased her and something he had cultivated as part of his charm. 'But first tell me . . . how are you?'

'Me?' She waved her hands and the sparkle of the diamonds

made flashes of light on the ceiling. 'I'm an old woman, Chris, but I can't complain. I'm very well and thanks to you, I am happy with Miss Oldhill. We are already great friends. She reads beautifully and she is so quiet and calm. This is something I need – quiet and calm. I must tell you: she bought me a present. I sent her out shopping yesterday – her clothes were ... well, never mind. I sent her out shopping and she thought of me. She gave me the Beethoven piano trios – Kempff, Szeryng and Fournier.' She smiled happily at Patterson. 'Kempff! What a master! I spent most of the morning in bed listening ... I can't thank you enough, Chris, for finding her for me.'

'I thought she was right for you,' Patterson said, a little stunned that Sheila should have done this.

There was more chit-chat, then he laid the transfers on the table and she signed them. Her signature was a blind scrawl, but he was used to that. Then he handed over $5,000 in $100 bills.

'You asked for this, Mrs Morely-Johnson.'

The old lady took the money and stowed it away in her hand-bag.

'I am always needing cash and Miss Oldhill explained to me that I should have cash in my bag ... that's right, isn't it, Chris?'

Patterson hesitated.

'A cheque is safer.' So it was Sheila who had sold this idea to the old lady. 'Still, you have it now.'

Mrs Morely-Johnson tapped his wrist with her long fingers.

'You mustn't treat me like a child.'

Patterson forced a laugh.

'The last thing in the world I would think of doing.' His mind suddenly uneasy. He knew he had been treating this old lady like a child. He had been in complete control of her money and now this sudden discordant note.

'I mustn't waste more of your time, Chris,' Mrs Morely-Johnson was saying. 'I am also keeping Bromhead waiting. Life is such a rush, isn't it? I have a lot of shopping to do.' Again she patted Patterson's wrist. 'Some time next week you must dine with me. I will ask Sheila to call you.'

'I would like that very much.'

Patterson got to his feet. He felt uneasy and frustrated. He had no excuse to see Sheila. As he went out into the lobby he found Jack Bromhead standing by the front door: immaculate in his uniform, his cockaded hat under his arm. He gave Patterson a slight bow and opened the front door for him.

'Morning, Mr Patterson,' he said in his beautifully modulated voice. 'Did you find madam well?'

Patterson, always conscious that underlings were important, gave Bromhead his warm smile.

'She looks wonderful,' he said, slightly raising his voice in the hope Mrs Morely-Johnson might hear him. 'What a great personality!'

Bromhead inclined his head, seeing through Patterson's act and going along with it.

'You are right, sir . . . a remarkable personality.'

Mrs Morely-Johnson listened. What dear men these two were! she thought.

As Patterson left the elevator, feeling frustrated and not a little worried, he saw Sheila at the bookstall, buying a copy of *Life*. This was no accidental meeting. Bromhead had arranged it and his timing had been perfect. Listening at the door, and when he had heard Mrs Morely-Johnson telling Patterson she had shopping to do, he had signalled to Sheila who had left the penthouse and had taken the elevator to the lobby. She had gone to the bookstall and had glanced through the magazines, watching the lighted indicator that told her the elevator was returning to the penthouse. Then when she saw the elevator was descending, she selected *Life* magazine and was paying for it as Patterson came out of the cage.

She turned and walked towards him, leafing through the magazine, apparently unaware that she was approaching him.

'Sheila.'

She paused, then looked up.

'Why . . . Chris.' She gave him a ghost of a smile. 'I was hoping to have a word with you.' She moved closer to him. 'I wanted to thank you for . . .'

'Never mind that,' Patterson said, his breathing uneven. 'Let's take the thanks as written. The old lady will be down in a few minutes. When do I see you, Sheila?'

The smoky blue eyes opened wide.

'See me? Why . . . you're seeing me now.'

Was she conning him? Patterson wondered. *But I pay my debts.* She had said that. What was this? He stared at her, trying to see any sign of promise, but the calm face and now the spectacles and the severe hair-do which he had suggested presented a baffling barrier to him, but he was sure still, if he pressed the right button, she was there to be had.

'I would like to take you out again.'

'That's very kind of you.'

There was a long pause while he waited hopefully but as he realized she wasn't adding to this impersonal statement, he said, 'Fine. I know a very good restaurant not far from here. When can you fix it?'

'I don't know. I'm not free now. I'll call you.'

'You get a day off ... the other one had Sundays. Suppose we make it next Sunday?'

'It's very nice of you, but I may have things to do on my day off. I don't know.' She gave him the faint smile again. 'I'll call you. I must go. While Mrs Morely-Johnson is out, I have a lot of things to do for her. I'll call you.' She moved around him, lifting her hand in a little wave of farewell, then she entered the elevator and the doors closed.

Patterson walked thoughtfully across the lobby, ignoring the doorman who saluted him and went down to his car.

While Mrs Morely-Johnson was entertaining friends in the hotel grill-room, Sheila was eating a chicken sandwich in the penthouse office. She was occupied with Mrs Morely-Johnson's mail which was considerable. There were a number of begging letters to be answered. Mrs Morely-Johnson was generous but she insisted that every applicant should be investigated before she decided to give or refuse and this meant a lot of work.

As Sheila was reaching for another letter, she heard the front door click open. Only she and Bromhead had keys to the penthouse, so she sat back, putting the letter down and waited.

Bromhead came into the room. He was wearing his uniform and the sight of him gave her confidence. This man was a professional. Not once during the brief time she had talked to him had she seen him out of character in his role as a kindly, efficient servant.

He sat down in a chair opposite Sheila's desk.

'You saw Patterson?'

'Yes.' Briefly she described the meeting and Bromhead nodded approvingly.

'Very good ... keep him dangling. Don't call him until Friday evening, then tell him you have found time to go out with him.'

'I was going to do that.'

Bromhead again nodded his approval. She was, like himself, a professional, he thought. All she needed was a little nudge, a touch on the steering wheel, and she reacted immediately in the right way.

'He takes his women to the Star motel,' Bromhead told her. 'It is safe and discreet – twenty miles out of town. It's a place where no questions are asked. Would you go with him to the motel if he asks you on Sunday?'

She shook her head.

'Not yet ... it's too soon.'

'I agree. The thing that is good about this operation is we have time. When you think the time is right, let me know.' He looked suddenly sharply at her. 'Don't let him rush you off your feet. He has a lot of appeal. The stage must be set before he goes into action ... I don't have to tell you that.'

She stared fixedly at him.

'No man rushes me off my feet,' she said.

'All right. I just mentioned it.' He paused, then went on, 'And Gerald?'

'I haven't heard from him yet, but I will. I gave him seventy dollars.' She looked away from Bromhead. 'He worries me.'

'He worries me too. He is unreliable. I think he is too stupid to realize what really big money means, but he is essential. I wish he wasn't, but without him, we put down the shutters.' Bromhead frowned down at his square, clean fingernails. 'What we have to be careful about is that he doesn't get involved with another woman. You musn't neglect him.'

Sheila picked up a pen and made an impatient squiggle on a letter, lying on her desk.

'You don't have to tell me, but with Patterson, it will be difficult. I can only get away on Sundays and Sundays I must keep for Patterson.'

'The old lady is always in bed by eleven. You could see Gerald when she has gone to sleep.'

Sheila considered this, then shook her head.

'It's too risky. If she woke and called me ... it could ruin everything.'

'You are a nurse ... there are such things as sleeping pills.'

She looked up.

'Is that what you think I should do?'

'It's a suggestion.'

Again she thought, then again she shook her head.

'No. I can't meet Gerald in town. We could be seen.'

Bromhead nodded. Looking ahead, planning, making decisions, taking risks, moving forward, withdrawing were now part of his life.

'Gerald has a car. Do you think it would be too risky to meet him in some car park not far from here and he could take you somewhere?'

She lifted her shoulders.

'Do you?'

Bromhead thought of what was involved. If Sheila and Gerald were seen together and remembered and if there was an inquiry later and someone talked the whole plan could explode, and yet he knew it was essential that she kept control not only of Patterson but also of Gerald.

'We must take some risks, but we must minimize them as far as possible.' He paused to think while Sheila waited, confident he would solve any problem. 'First, the hotel staff must get to know you. They must accept you as they accept me – part of the hotel background. To do this you must make several trips a day down to the lobby, to the bookstall, to mail letters, to buy stamps. You must think up some reason to speak to the hall porter and the doorman. That I can leave to you but establish yourself so the staff regard you as one of themselves. There's a staircase from here, reached through your bedroom. It leads down to the 19th floor. You may not have noticed the exit door. It is behind a curtain. It's there in case of fire. The door is bolted on the inside so you can get out quickly. You must buy a blonde wig. Get yourself a drab-looking dustcoat. Leave here by the staircase, then take the elevator down from the 19th floor. After eleven o'clock the elevator goes on automatic. The night staff in the lobby won't know if you are staying at the hotel or visiting someone. The trick with this is to show confidence. Leave the elevator and walk briskly across the lobby and out. You do the same in reverse when you return. Don't hesitate. You won't be noticed. Take the elevator to the 19th floor, walk up the stairs and enter your room. You need do this only twice a week. Before leaving, give the old lady a sleeping pill. How you do that is your business. Seeing Gerald twice a week should keep him happy. What do you think?'

She thought about this, then nodded.

'Yes.'

'All right.' He got to his feet. 'How do you find the old lady?'

'She's very easy ... I like her.'

Bromhead paused in the open doorway.

'Don't get to like her too much ... no one lasts for ever.'

When he had gone, Sheila got up and went to the big window

and looked down at the luxury yachts in the harbour. The sun turned the water into an oily rainbow.

Perhaps the air conditioner was making her feel cold. She shivered. Opening the terrace door she went out into the hot sunshine. Looking down at the town, the sea and the busy traffic, she still felt cold.

Gerald rolled off her with a moan of satisfaction. She knew there would be no after-play and she was thankful. Gerald was so selfish and adolescent, once satisfied, he wanted only to sleep. She waited until his breathing became heavy, then she reached for the towel and wiped his sweat off her body. She longed to take a shower, but she didn't want to wake him so she lay still, feeling the heat of his body as they nearly touched on the narrow, sordid bed and she stared up at the dirty white ceiling, lit by the flashing neon sign from the night-club across the way.

The room was small and insufferably hot. Through the open window came the sounds of the waterfront: drunken voices, squeals from excited girls, the blare of transistor radios and the shuffling of feet.

This, she reminded herself, she would have to endure twice a week. Even then, she couldn't be sure that he wouldn't look for another woman. She had known when they had teamed up that he would present problems. He just didn't understand nor ever would appreciate what it meant to have unlimited money – as she did and Bromhead did. His mind was too small. The only thing that bothered him was boredom. Give him enough money with which to eat, drink, run a car, go every night to some night-club, dance with some attractive girl, have sex with her, yak with kids of his own age and he would be happy. But she was determined to make him understand; determined to mould him; determined to teach him the power of money. But there were moments like this, as she lay by his side, listening to his snorting as he slept that she wondered uneasily how long she could keep him in her control. Bromhead kept saying: *Time is on our side. This is a long term operation.* But it wasn't for her. Clever as he was, Bromhead didn't seem to realize her difficulties. There were times when she felt uneasy about Bromhead because he had more confidence in her than she had in herself. She knew she had this magic that attracted men, but to have to endure the lust of a boy like Gerald now made her skin crawl, but Gerald was the focal point of this operation. Without him, it seemed to her now that there would be no future for her and no money. Money? Bromhead had said in his quiet unemotional voice there could be a million and a half dollars, split between the three of them.

In the flashing light of the neon sign, she looked at the blonde wig lying on the dressing-table.

Bromhead was clever, she thought. His idea about the wig and the dustcoat had worked. She had had no trouble meeting Gerald in the parking lot behind the hotel and she was confident she would have no trouble returning to her room in the penthouse. Nor was she worried that Mrs Morely-Johnson wouldn't sleep through the night. The pill she had dropped into the glass of hot milk as the old lady settled in bed would keep her asleep until the morning.

But there was still this problem of Gerald. He had gaped at her through the Volkswagen window, not recognizing her in the blonde wig, then when she spoke, he had suddenly grinned.

'I like you blonde, baby. You give me hot ideas.'

She was shocked with the room he had found for himself, but she was careful not to tell him so. It was on the top floor of a rooming house in a back street off the waterfront. It was cheap, and he explained that with only seventy dollars a week coming in, who cares about a room? This worried her. He had such a low standard of living and he thought small. He seemed content to live like an animal: even some animals would be more fussy than he.

He had complained as he drove her to the rooming house that he was so goddamn bored.

'This is a hell of a town. It's okay if you have money. Everything costs! There's nothing to do! How long is this thing going on?'

This she didn't know. If only she had enough money to give him so he could go to Los Angeles where he could amuse himself, find a girl and come back when it was time. But there was no money. He had to make do with seventy dollars a week.

Lying on the bed, listening to his moaning and snorting as he slept, she wondered if she could control him if this thing went on for weeks, and if she was to believe Bromhead, it could.

Moving slowly, she edged off the bed and stood up. Gerald muttered something, then began to snort again. She went into the shower room, turned on the cold water and filled the basin. She dipped the towel into the water and then wiped her body. The cold feel of the towel was a relief but the moisture immediately dried in the suffocating heat of the tiny room. She dressed. Moving to the window, she looked at her watch in the flashing light of the neon sign. It was 01.15. She had a long walk along the waterfront to the Plaza Beach Hotel. She wouldn't be back until after 02.00, but she felt it was useless to wake Gerald. He would only complain if she asked him to drive her back. The thought that she would have to face this chore twice a week made her flinch, but the pay-off would be worth it, she told herself.

She put on the blonde wig, then the dustcoat. She had to be sure the wig covered her dark hair so she turned on the light to look in the small mirror above the dressing-table. She had to make quick adjustments, then she snapped off the light, but the light had woken Gerald.

He sat up.

'What the hell's going on?' he demanded querulously.

'Go to sleep, Gerry. It's all right. I'm leaving.'

'What's the time?'

'After one.'

He fumbled for the switch of the bedside lamp and turned the light on. Sitting up, naked, he looked young and defenceless as he blinked at her.

'Man! That blonde wig! I really dig for it!' He threw off the sheet and struggled off the bed. 'I'll drive you back.'

'No ... you sleep. I'll walk.'

He pulled on his hipsters.

'Is that what you think of me?' He paused to stare at her. 'You think I'm such a goddamn creep I'd let you walk all that way?'

'No.' She felt a sudden weakness surge through her. 'I think you should sleep.'

'What else have I got to do in this goddamn town except sleep?' He dragged a grubby sweater over his head. 'You do think I'm a creep, don't you?'

'No, Gerry.'

He came to her and put his arms around her, pulling her close to him. Forcing herself, she put her arms around him and her face against his. They stood for some moments holding on to each other, then she felt a pang of desire run through her and she tightened her grip.

'I know I'm a creep,' he said, his hands sliding down her back and cupping her buttocks. 'I know it, but you're the best thing that has ever happened to me. You want money. Okay, so you want money ... money to me means nothing but trouble. I don't want trouble ... I want you.'

She ran her fingers through his thick, unwashed hair.

'I must go, Gerry.'

He released her and opened the door.

'Okay ... then let's go.'

Although she was aching for sleep, knowing she would have to cope with Patterson the following day, she felt she had to show her gratitude for the nicest thing he had ever said to her. *I want you.* No other man had said this to her. *I love you.* Many, many times ... but what did that mean? Love? Nothing! But I want you, that was something.

She took off the dustcoat and let it drop to the floor.

'You have me in the mood, Gerry,' she said, pushed the door shut and held out her arms to him, smiling.

A little numbed and sick with tiredness and as he drove her back to the Plaza Beach Hotel, she remembered her father saying so often: *What you put in, you take out.*

Read one way, it was a dirty snigger: read another way, it was a philosophy of life.

The Coq d'Or restaurant was situated some ten miles from town and was considered one of the better class restaurants on this strip of the Pacific coast.

On Sundays it was crowded, but the people who dined there weren't the type Patterson knew. His people would shun such a place. He was confident he ran no risk coming here and he was always careful where he took his girl friends. He was acutely aware that any gossip reaching the bank's ears could be detrimental to his career.

Sheila had telephoned him on an outside line just before he was leaving the bank on Friday evening. She told him she would be free to see him at 18.00 Sunday evening.

The sound of her quiet voice sent a stab of desire through him. He said he would pick her up in the lobby of the Splendid Hotel. Although he didn't spell it out, he was nervous that the Plaza Beach Hotel's doorman might gossip.

He found her waiting in the lobby. She was wearing the white dress again, but she now had a touch of lipstick and her hair was dressed becomingly and yet, Patterson felt she was still remote and the barrier was still there.

He had to concentrate on his driving as the Sunday evening traffic was heavy and they only exchanged pleasantries about how hot it was, did she like the hotel and how was Mrs Morely-Johnson? ... that kind of talk.

He had reserved a corner table at the Coq d'Or restaurant and he suggested because of the crowd in the bar they should have drinks at their table. Although it was only just after 19.00, people were already dancing. The four piece band played softly but with a good, sharp rhythm.

The *maître d'hôtel* fussed over them. Champagne cocktails arrived. Patterson told the *maître d'hôtel* he would order later.

When they were settled with their drinks, Sheila looked around.

'It's nice here ... the band is marvellous.'

Patterson wasn't interested in the band. He looked hungrily at her.

'How are things?' he asked. 'Are you happy?'

She nodded.

'Yes, thank you. Mrs Morely-Johnson is so nice. She seems to like me.'

'Yes ... she's a funny old thing. She has moods. You must watch out ... sometimes she can be tricky.'

Sheila sipped her drink, not looking at him.

'But most people are like that.' She abruptly looked up, staring at him. 'Of course, I realize it is early days yet.'

'Yes.' Patterson gave her his warm smile. 'Let me alert you. I know all the signs. When she is in a bad mood, she fidgets with her bracelets and hums under her breath. These are warning signs. When she starts this performance, watch out. You must go along with anything she says. You understand? Never try to persuade her to do anything ... just go along with her. I tell you this because it could be useful.'

She nodded, turning the cocktail glass in her fingers.

'Thank you.'

He leaned back, pleased and very sure of himself.

'I've known her for something like four years and I've always been able to handle her ... even in her worst moments.'

She sipped her drink before saying, 'But then she is in love with you.'

Startled, Patterson stared at her. Then he realized she was stating a fact and he smiled, passing his hand over his immaculately groomed hair.

'Not quite, but perhaps something like that,' he conceded. 'If she was twenty years younger I would have to be careful,' and he laughed.

There was a pause, then Sheila said, 'You have, of course, an irresistible appeal to women.'

Patterson leaned back in his chair. Coming from her, this meant something to him. He knew he did have an appeal to women, but she was the first woman to have told him so. He finished his drink, then gave her a wry grimace.

'Perhaps to most women ... but not to you.'

She looked beyond him at the dancers, jammed together on the tiny dance floor.

'What makes you think that?'

He fidgeted with a fork: picking it up, staring at it and putting it down.

Trying to keep his voice casual, he said, 'I feel there's a barrier between us ... you're so impersonal.'

She regarded him for a long moment, then she pushed back her chair and stood up.

'Shall we dance?'

Although there was little space for dancing, she moved beautifully and her body, pressed against his, gave him a sensual pleasure he hadn't before experienced. As they danced, she touched his neck very lightly with cool finger-tips to send hot blood surging through him.

When they returned to their table, the *maître d'hôtel* arrived.

Without consulting her, Patterson ordered king-sized prawns to be followed by creamed chicken breasts in rice and truffles.

'The Pouilly-Fumé, I think, Jean ... unless you have better ideas?'

'That would be perfect, Mr Patterson.' The *maître d'hôtel* bowed and went away.

'You are very experienced,' Sheila said.

Patterson looked pleased. Praise to him was like water to a plant.

'Well, you know...' He waved a deprecating hand. 'You dance beautifully ... I really mean that.'

'So do you.'

There was a long pause, then he said, 'But you must admit there's a barrier between us.'

She shook her head.

'Chris ... please don't expect too much from me so quickly.' She put her cool hand on his. 'We are not going to die tomorrow. I get the feeling you can't wait for anything. I happen to be the waiting type. I have to think, probe and move carefully. Will you try to understand?'

His blood on fire, Patterson gripped her hand.

'But we could die tomorrow. It's the pattern of things. For me, life is urgent as it should be for you. Driving back tonight, we could be hit by a truck. How can you say we won't die tomorrow? We could die tonight! Don't you feel we are all living on borrowed time? I believe I should do everything I want to do now ... grab at every opportunity for it may be too late to wait.'

She drew her hand away.

'Don't you believe in destiny? What is to be ... will be?'

Patterson moved impatiently.

'I don't believe in waiting. Yes ... I believe in destiny, but I also believe I can cheat destiny by not waiting.'

The prawns arrived and they waited while the wine was poured, tasted and approved and the waiter had moved away.

'I understand,' Sheila said as they began to shell the prawns, 'but please be patient, Chris. I move slowly – I'm made like that. For us to be as intimate as we will be – for me, I need time.' Then she smiled at him.

For the first time he had known her and desired her, the smoky blue eyes were no longer remote. There was that sexual thing coming from her that made his heartbeat quicken and that turned his mouth dry.

Four

While Mrs Morely-Johnson was playing bridge on the terrace with three of her friends, Bromhead opened the front door of the penthouse and, crossing the vestibule, entered Sheila's office. He had come because, as she was getting into the Rolls with Mrs Morely-Johnson that morning, she had whispered that she must see him.

He found her waiting for him, sitting at her desk. This day was Saturday, close on a week since she had seen Patterson. Each time Patterson had come to the penthouse she had avoided him. It had been Bromhead who had opened the door.

Bromhead had had little chance of talking to Sheila until now, but looking at her as he stood in the doorway, he saw she was under a strain.

'Shut the door,' she said abruptly.

He did as he was told, then came over to the chair by the desk and sat down.

'Something wrong?'

'We can't wait any longer,' she said. 'Your bright idea of the wig and the dustcoat has come unstuck. Last night when I returned from seeing Gerald, the house detective stopped me and asked where I was going. I was lucky. The elevator doors were open. I pushed by him and shut the doors before he could reach me. Of course he knew by the indicator I had got out on the 19th floor. When I reached my room, I went to the elevator and saw it descend, then come up to the 19th floor. He had come up – looking for me. You will have to get rid of the wig and the coat, Jack. This could be dangerous.'

Bromhead grimaced. He saw that at once. Joe Handley, the night detective was smart – perhaps over smart. Bromhead should have thought of him. Bromhead knew there were only four elderly couples living in suites on the 19th floor – people who certainly wouldn't be interested in a young, blonde woman at 02.00. Yet this blonde woman had gone up to the 19th floor and then had vanished. It was the kind of mystery that Handley would dig into: the kind of mystery he wouldn't leave alone nor forget.

But fortunately he only came on duty at 21.00 and went off duty at 07.00 so he wasn't likely to see Sheila without her wig. The day detective, Fred Lawson, who had been with the hotel for years was fat, lazy and stupid, but if ever Handley saw Sheila during the day, he might recognize her, blonde wig or no blonde wig. There were danger signals here.

'Gerald is driving me crazy,' Sheila went on. 'He's so demanding. Now he wants to see me every night. He is stupidly jealous of Patterson. He has nothing to do during the day. The money I give him doesn't last a week. We can't wait any longer. I intend to tell Patterson I'm ready.'

'But this is a long-term operation,' Bromhead said uneasily. 'I warned you about this. Rush it and we could spoil it.'

'It's all right for you to talk.' Even under stress, Sheila remained calm. 'You don't have to handle Gerald nor Patterson ... but I do. I am sure I can handle Patterson now. I'm sure of it ... we can't wait any longer.'

Bromhead hesitated, then shrugged.

'All right. Then tomorrow?'

'Yes.' She looked at her desk clock. 'He could be in now,' and she dialled Patterson's home number. There was a long pause while the ringing tone sounded, then just as she was about to hang up, she heard Patterson's voice: querulous and sharp.

'Yes? Who is it?'

'You sound cross, Chris. Have I interrupted you?'

Bromhead nodded with approval. What an artist this woman was! he thought. The sensual caress in her soft voice had an effect even on him.

'Sheila' Patterson's voice became all charm. 'I've been waiting to hear from you. I haven't seen you all the week.' She could hear his breathing, quick, short and uneven. 'I was just off for a round of golf. What have you been doing with yourself?'

'Things...' She paused, then went on, 'Can we meet tomorrow?'

'Of course. Would you like to go to the Coq d'Or again?'

Again she deliberately paused.

'I thought, Chris ... something more intimate. A smoked salmon sandwich and you.'

She heard him draw in a sharp breath.

'You really mean that?'

'Chris ... please...'

'I'll fix it. Let's meet at the same place and time.'

'Yes ... and Chris, where will you be taking me?'

'There's a motel I know. It's nice and you'll like it.' She looked at Bromhead.

'Would that be the Star motel, Chris?'

'You know it?' His voice sounded startled.

'We went for a drive yesterday and passed it. I thought it looked wonderful.'

'It is ... you'll love it. I'll fix everything. Sheila...'

'No more now,' she said firmly. 'Then at six.'

'Marvellous ... wonderful ... terrific!'

She replaced the receiver.

'The Star motel?' Bromhead asked.

She nodded.

'You did very well. I'll be there at seven o'clock,' he said. 'Hold him off until then ... you understand?'

'Yes.'

They looked at each other.

'If it wasn't for that little bastard,' Bromhead said, 'I would be certain this is going to work out, but with him in the background, we can't be too careful.'

'We can't be too careful anyway. That detective worries me.'

'Forget him ... it's a natural hazard. It's my fault. I should have remembered him.' Bromhead got to his feet. 'Let's fix Patterson first. Next week we'll have to decide what to do with Gerald. You won't be able to see him at night now,' Bromhead paused while he thought. 'I hate wasting money but it could be the solution to get him out of town until we are ready to use him. We could send him to L.A. With five hundred dollars, he could keep himself amused, couldn't he?'

'I've thought of that, but now, I don't think he'll go. He has this thing about me ... this has built up. Now he's jealous of Patterson. He talks about money meaning nothing and I'm all he wants. Anyway, where do we find five hundred dollars?'

'I'll find it,' Bromhead said, thinking of Solly Marks. 'I think I'd better talk to Gerald.' He looked up and for the first time since Sheila had known him, he slid out of character. His thin face tightened and his eyes turned into chips of grey ice. Suddenly this was a face of utter ruthlessness ... a killer's face and it sent a chill through Sheila.

'No! You must leave him to me,' she said. 'You don't know him as I do. He has to be persuaded ... not forced. He's like an obstinate child.'

The benign, kindly expression came back into Bromhead's eyes. Once more he was the efficient, dignified chauffeur.

'Let's fix Patterson first. You will leave here just before six tomorrow?'

'Yes.'

'Before then I'll let you have the bug. It's a limpet job and small. You can stick it on any flat surface ... under the night table would do.'

She nodded.

'You're doing fine,' he said, moving to the door. 'You leave the worrying to me. Make a parcel of the wig and the coat. I'll get rid of them tomorrow.'

As Bromhead crossed the hotel lobby to go to his room across the courtyard, Fred Lawson, the hotel detective, appeared from nowhere and rested his big, fat hand on Bromhead's arm. Bromhead regarded him, his thin face expressionless, then said, 'Hello, Fred ... you want me?'

Lawson was a massively built man with thinning black hair,

small cunning eyes and a mouth that could serve as a mouse-trap.

'Got a moment, Jack?'

'Just going to watch the ball game on TV ... what is it?'

'This won't take long,' and Lawson steered him down a corridor and into his tiny office. 'Just wanted to ask you something.' He sat down behind his desk and waved Bromhead to a chair. 'You know anything about a tall, well-built woman, blonde, around thirty years of age who wears a fawn dustcoat?'

Bromhead felt his nerve ends prickle, but his benign expression merely shifted to a look of inquiry.

'I know a number of blondes,' he said and smiled, 'but I don't know about a dustcoat.' His mind was working swiftly. This was dangerous. Pretend ignorance and he was sure Handley wouldn't leave it alone and would keep prodding Lawson to press for an inquiry. If this was reported to the Director of the hotel it could become dynamite. 'Why ask me, Fred?'

Lawson scowled.

'It's Handley ... that guy will give me an ulcer if he goes on the way he goes on. He says he saw a woman use the elevator at two o'clock this morning, going up to the 19th floor. She was youngish, blonde and wearing a fawn dustcoat. He challenged her but she avoided him and beat him to the elevator. He went right up after her, but she'd vanished. I've checked the 19th and the 18th floors, but no one knows anything about her. So that could leave the penthouse. Handley wants me to talk to the old lady, but I thought I'd better have a word with you first. The old lady wouldn't like it ... would she?'

'You're right.' Bromhead had already made up his mind, he went on. 'I told her it was risky, but she wanted to be kind. I'm sorry, Fred. I should have stopped it, but at the time, I didn't see anything really wrong ...'

Lawson gaped at him.

'Told who? What are you talking about?'

'Miss Oldhill, of course. Now look, Fred, she's new here and the old lady likes her and ...'

Lawson waved his fat hand.

'Wait a minute. You mean the new companion ... Oldhill? That her name?'

'Yes. She has a girl-friend ... the one with the dustcoat. This girl was passing through on her way to L.A. and she dropped off to see Oldhill. The girl's short of money ... who isn't? On the bus, she picked up a boy who wanted to show her the town.

She asked Oldhill if she could share her bed for the night to save a hotel check. Oldhill asked me. I told her the hotel wouldn't go for it, but if the girl slipped in and out ... who would know? My mistake, Fred. I didn't reckon on Handley being so sharp. Sorry about it ... can't say more, can I?'

Lawson breathed heavily as he frowned at Bromhead.

'Dead against the rules, Jack. You could get me into trouble. You should know better.'

Bromhead knew his man. He knew Lawson lived by graft.

'You're right. If you can forget it, Fred ... I'll remember it.' He paused, then went on, 'I was talking to the old lady only yesterday. Believe it or not, she didn't know there was a house detective in the hotel. She was asking what she should do about the staff – extra service. I told her I'd think about it.' Bromhead smiled at Lawson. 'You forget ... I remember ... right?'

But Lawson frowned down at his fat hands. Bromhead could almost hear his brain creak as he thought. Finally, he said, 'I don't know, Jack. Handley's a sonofabitch. How do I fix him?'

Bromhead had already solved that problem.

'Tell him you checked with the old lady and she told you the girl was her guest.'

Lawson's fat face brightened.

'Yeah ... that's an idea. Okay, Jack, you see me right ... I'll see you right.'

'The old lady gives me the money for the staff. Why should you wait?' Bromhead took out his billfold, extracted a hundred dollar bill and slid it over to Lawson. 'How's this, Fred?'

The bill disappeared as Lawson's fat fingers snapped it up.

'Sure, Jack, but tell this Oldhill broad not to do it again. That sort of thing could lose me my job.'

'She won't. I'll talk to her.'

'The other broad still up there?'

'She caught the 7.30 bus. Maybe you weren't in the lobby.'

Lawson who had been eating a full-scale breakfast in his office at that time, shook his head.

'That's right ... I wasn't around.'

'Well, she's gone.' Bromhead got to his feet. 'See you, Fred, and thanks. Christmas is coming. I'll see you right with the old lady. She can be generous at Christmas.'

When Joe Handley reported for duty that evening, Lawson who was his superior tramped over him.

'Listen to me, Joe ... you can act too smart,' he said, glaring at Handley. 'Okay, so you keep your eyes open, but watch it ...

use your head. I checked with Mrs Morely-Johnson. That woman you've been yelling about was a guest of hers. Mrs Morely-Johnson didn't like me checking. She's touchy ... so watch it in the future.'

Handley stared at Lawson.

'She went to the 19th floor,' he said quietly. 'Why didn't she go direct to the penthouse?'

Lawson hadn't thought of this, but he was committed, so he blustered.

'Cut it out! I've talked to the old lady. If she's happy, you be happy!'

'This woman went up the stairs to the fire door ... is that it?'

'I said cut it out!' Lawson growled. 'Get moving! You should be on duty!'

Then Handley knew someone had bribed Lawson. He filed the blonde woman away in his cop mind for future reference.

The light coming through the half-open door of the shower room faintly lit the comfortable furnished motel bedroom; the rest of the room was in darkness.

The big double bed was in the darkest part of the room and only the red gleam of two burning cigarettes told that two people lay on the bed. The noise of the heavy Sunday traffic on the highway just penetrated through the double glazing: the air conditioner hummed softly: there was no discordant sound.

Patterson lay limp and satiated. His mind dwelt on the past half hour. This woman, lying naked by his side, had been everything he had hoped for. No ... that wasn't true: she had been better than his most sensual expectations. This was an experienced woman who knew how to give and receive pleasure. In a drowsy stupor, he thought back on his many sexual encounters. Nothing he had known could be compared with the past half hour. He dragged hard on his cigarette, drawing smoke down into his lungs: his patient wait had been more than rewarded.

'Chris ... what is the time?' Sheila asked out of the darkness.

This was a jarring note to Patterson. Who the hell cared about time right now? He peered at the luminous hands of his watch.

'Just after half past seven ... why?'

'I must be back by eleven.'

Why must women talk at a moment like this? he thought. They always did. Women never seemed to know when to stop talking. Didn't they ever realize that after a body shattering explosion like the one he had just experienced, a man wanted to rest, doze and dream it all over again?

'You'll be back in time.' He stubbed out his cigarette, then closed his eyes. They had two and a half hours before they need to think of the hotel. If she would only let him doze for a while, in half an hour or so, he would then be able to show her what love making really meant.

'Was it good for you, Chris?'

'It was marvellous.'

He remained quiet, his eyes closed. Maybe she would stop talking and doze too, but she didn't.

'Was it the best ever, Chris? It was for me.'

He resigned himself. She was going to talk and he had to put up with it.

'Yes ... the best ever.'

A pause, then she said, 'Would you say something for me?'

'What?' He tried to control the impatience in his voice, but didn't quite succeed.

'Please say this: I, Chris Patterson, considers Sheila Oldhill the best lay he has ever had.'

The ideas women get! he thought.

'Look, darling, I'd like to sleep a little. Then we can start this all over again. How about it?'

'Say it for me, please, Chris. I want to hear you say it, then we'll sleep ... I promise.'

God! Women! he thought, then for the sake of peace, he intoned without much enthusiasm, 'I, Christopher Patterson, thinks Sheila Oldhill the most marvellous, wonderful and exciting woman I have ever slept with. How's that?'

Thinking of Bromhead with his tape recorder, sitting in his Mini-Austin Cooper Mrs Morely-Johnson had given him as a runabout, Sheila was satisfied.

'Thank you, darling. Maybe I'm a little stupid, but I did want to hear you say that ... now go to sleep.'

Patterson drifted off into a light sleep while Sheila waited. She let him sleep for half an hour, then she got off the bed and took a shower. She thought of Bromhead waiting out there.

'Don't rush anything,' he had said as he had given her the microphone. 'Remember ... this is a chance in a lifetime.'

As she came out of the shower room, leaving the door wide open so the light brightened the shadows of the bedroom, Patterson woke. He sat up.

'What are you up to?'

'I've had a shower.' She came across the room, naked with the light behind her and he felt desire for her rise in him.

'Come here.'

'Chris ... I want to talk to you.'

'Not now ... come here.'

She put on the bathrobe the motel supplied.

'Chris ... do you realize how dangerous this is and do you realize it can't happen again?'

'What do you mean ... dangerous?'

'Dangerous to you.'

'Oh, come on, Sheila. You mean the bank? Nonsense. This place is a hundred per cent safe.'

'I don't mean the bank. I mean Mrs Morely-Johnson.'

'Dangerous? What's all this, Sheila?'

'She's in love with you.'

'Oh, nonsense. I know she's a sexy old thing. In her heyday, she had lovers by the dozens, but now she's seventy-eight, for God's sake!' Patterson laughed. 'Of course she regards me as her Prince Charming, but that means nothing ... to me. I go along with her. I have to: it's part of my job. I don't mind telling you when she turns girlish she bores me sick.' He suddenly realized he was talking too much. 'Come here, darling. We're wasting time.'

'There's time.' She came over to the bed and sat on it, keeping away from him. She wasn't sure about the strength of the microphone although Bromhead had assured her that it would pick up every sound in the cabin. 'If she ever found out about us, it would hurt her. You realize that, Chris?'

'How could she find out? This isn't the time for this kind of talk.' He switched on the bedside lamp and half raised himself to stare at her. She had gone remote on him. Her quiet, calm expression had come back and he realized her barrier had come up again between them. For no reason he could quite put his finger on, he began to feel uneasy. 'What's the matter, Sheila?'

'I don't understand you,' she said. 'I have seen you with the old lady. Are you acting all the time? You are so nice to her ... so charming ... yet you say she bores you sick.'

'Do we have to discuss this stupid old woman right now?' Patterson demanded, losing patience. 'Come here! I want you!'

'Do you think she's stupid?'

'Well, don't you?' Patterson was becoming exasperated. 'Do

you want me to spell it out? At the age of seventy-eight, she is vain, half blind, gushing and she can't keep her eyes off young men. If you don't call that stupid ... then what do you call it?'

Sheila drew in a long breath. If she had written the script or if Bromhead had written it, it couldn't have been more word perfect.

Listening in his car outside the motel cabin, Bromhead decided he had what he wanted. He snapped down the stop button on the recorder, started the car engine, sounded his horn three times, in short loud blasts, then drove rapidly back to the Plaza Beach Hotel.

Sheila heard the horn blasts and she stood up. The first stage of the operation had been successfully completed, now came the more difficult stage.

'I'm hungry,' she said. 'Let's eat.'

She went over to the plastic bag that Patterson had brought, opened it and took from it two neatly packed parcels.

Patterson watched her. Why was he feeling uneasy? This woman had become so impersonal, so different from the moaning, thrashing woman who had clung to him, uttering little cries of pleasure as her finger-nails dug into his flesh.

Well, if she was hungry ... there was still plenty of time. He looked at his watch: 19.45. Yes ... it would be an idea to eat, then make love again. He too suddenly felt hungry.

She went to the refrigerator and took out the bottle of Chablis he had brought. He had already half drawn the cork. She poured the wine into glasses.

He lay still, watching her, wished she wasn't wearing the bathrobe.

'Take that off, Sheila,' he said. 'I want to see you.'

'Later.' She opened the packets and put one of them beside him, then she sat away from him with the other packet on her knee. 'Chris ... have you seen the old lady's will?' She began to eat the smoked salmon sandwich. "Her last will and testament ... that's what it's called, isn't it?'

He was reaching for a sandwich, but his hand paused.

'Will? Why bring that up?'

'I asked you a simple question: can't I have a simple answer?'

God! he thought, how remote she's become, and he became aware that he was lying naked on the bed. He shifted a little and pulled the sheet across him. Instinctively, he felt that there would be no more love making. He didn't know why except perhaps her calm remoteness told him this, but he was sure of it.

'I know nothing about her will,' he said. 'Why do you ask?'

'Does money mean anything to you?'

He began to get angry. There was a snap in his voice as he said, 'Of course it does ... doesn't it to you?'

'Yes.' There was a slight pause, then she said. 'You should know about her will.'

Patterson's face hardened. He felt at a disadvantage lying on the bed, half hidden by the sheet. He swung his legs off the bed and sat upright and looked directly at her.

He got no hint as to what was going on in her mind. She had this maddening remote look and she was eating the sandwich as if she were enjoying it.

'Sheila ... just what are you getting at?'

'You don't know she's leaving you a lot of money?'

'Me?' He stiffened, staring at her. 'A *lot* of money? How do you know?'

She finished the sandwich and reached for another. She could see he had become tense.

'She told me.'

'She told you she had left me money?' Patterson couldn't believe this. Sheila had been with the old lady for only eight days. The old lady had never hinted she was leaving him anything ... then why tell a new companion-help?

'Are you sure she told you, Sheila?'

'Why should I tell you if I wasn't sure?' She took another bite at the sandwich while she looked at him: cool, remote, the smoky blue eyes impersonal. 'Don't you believe me?'

'Frankly ... no!' He knew now for certain love making was finished. He wanted to get into his clothes. He didn't feel he could control this unexpected situation while he was naked. 'Wait a moment.'

Holding the sheet around him, he grabbed up his shirt, underpants and trousers and went into the shower room.

Sheila drank a little of the Chablis, then finished her second sandwich. Now, she told herself, she had to be careful. The fish was nibbling at the bait, but she had to judge the exact moment when to sink in the hook.

Patterson came out of the shower room. Sitting on the bed, he put on his socks and shoes. She watched him in silence.

When he had knotted his tie and had put on his jacket, she

said, 'Aren't you hungry, Chris? These sandwiches are delicious.'

He regarded her angrily and suspiciously.

'Just what is all this? Do you really mean the old lady told you she is leaving me a lot of money?'

She nodded.

'If you don't believe me ... why bother? Wait until she is dead, then you'll find out for yourself.'

He continued to stare at her, his mind busy. He hoped, of course, that Mrs Morely-Johnson would remember him in her will. Maybe ten thousand dollars ... something like that. But what did a *lot* of money mean? This old woman was worth five million dollars. She and he had always got along well together and he knew she was a bit sexy about him. If he could believe Sheila, this could mean real money. How he wanted that! Often, he had dreamed of leaving the bank and setting up as an independent broker. But he knew that was out of the question. You had to have substantial capital to set up on your own, but if he could be sure of getting a large sum ...

'She actually told you?' he said, trying to keep his voice steady.

'Why not look at her will? Then I don't have to convince you,' Sheila said quietly.

'Look at her will? I can't do that! You don't know what you are saying! Her will is with our Legal department! Of course, I can't look at it!'

Sheila finished her drink.

'You don't believe me and you can't look at her will ... then you must wait, mustn't you?'

Patterson began to sweat. He knew there would be no rest in his mind until he did know.'

'Just what did she tell you?'

Sheila studied him. She knew she had to be careful with him. She could goad him so far, but no further. He wasn't like Gerald: this man was shrewd, nimble-minded and experienced in tough business dealings. She felt this was the moment to sink in the gaff.

'She told me she was leaving you a hundred thousand dollars a year for life.'

Patterson drew in a hiss of breath and his hands turned into fists.

This couldn't be true! That was a fortune! She must have got it wrong!

'Wait a minute, Sheila! You mean ten thousand dollars, don't you? Ten thousand a year for life?'

The gaff was in, she thought.

'No, Chris. I know exactly what she said. One hundred thousand ... it's a lot of money, isn't it? You should be pleased.' she got to her feet, threw off the bathrobe and, naked, walked to where she had tossed off her clothes. Patterson didn't even see her. He was staring down at the carpet, his mind racing. God! If this were true! One hundred thousand dollars a year for life! He wouldn't even have to work again! He could travel! The women he could have! The fun he could have! London! Paris! Rome! The world would be at his feet.

He remained still, his mind in a whirl until Sheila touched him lightly on his shoulder. She was now dressed.

'Aren't you hungry? You've eaten nothing.'

Looking at him, she decided the difference between him and Gerald was he was greedy and Gerald was stupid.

Patterson stood up.

'Sheila! You must understand ... this is important to me,' he said, 'You really mean this? She really told you this?'

She turned away, went to the bedside table and pulled the limpet microphone free. She put it in its box and the box into her bag. Patterson was too preoccupied with his thoughts to notice what she was doing.

'Let's go back to the hotel, please,' she said and walked to the door.

She was sitting in the Wildcat by the time he had paid the check. He joined her, still in a daze. She noted with a wry smile that he hadn't pressed her to stay. As he drove her fast and in silence along the broad highway, she thought that maybe money meant more to men than sex. Men were realistic animals. Sex lasted for only a few minutes, but money, with luck and judgement, could last for ever.

As they approached the lights of Seaview boulevard, he said, 'Why did she tell you? That's something I can't understand. Just why did she tell you?'

'Why do women confide in each other?' Sheila said. 'Maybe, women are insecure ... even old women. They talk. They tell secrets. Perhaps she was so pleased to make you secure. She said how happy you had made her.'

Patterson could accept this.

'But why did she tell *you*?'

Sheila made a movement of impatience.

'Isn't this becoming a bore, Chris? I've told you what she told me. Why should I lie to you? Surely you can read the will?'

Could he? The will was with the Legal department of the bank. The legal man was Irving Fellows. He and Patterson didn't hit it off. Fellows was married with two children, serious and nothing in common with Patterson. Often, Patterson felt this thin, sour-faced lawyer disapproved of him. To see the will, he would have to get authorization from Mrs Morely-Johnson ... that was out of the question. He could never see the will.

'It's not possible,' he said.

'Then you must be satisfied that I'm telling you the truth.'

Why shouldn't he be satisfied? Patterson asked himself. Why should she lie to him? One hundred thousand dollars a year for life! If only Abe Weidman, the old lady's attorney had told him this, then he would believe it. Yet, now he wanted to believe it. But why should the old lady have told a new companion-help such a thing? The old girl was a little dotty. She might have confided to Sheila to boast. How can anyone read the mind of the rich and the dotty?

He pulled up outside the Splendid Hotel. He had to force his mind away from the thought of all this money to get out of the car and open the offside door.

Sheila slid out.

'It was wonderful,' she said. 'Thank you, Chris.'

His mind still far away, Patterson went through the motions. He touched her hand and turned on his charm.

'The greatest,' he said. 'Then next Sunday?'

'Yes ... I'd love that.' She took from her handbag the box containing the limpet microphone and put the box in his hand. 'A little memento, Chris, for a lovely evening.'

She touched his cheek lightly with her finger-tips, then turning, she walked quickly along the brightly lit boulevard to the Plaza Beach Hotel.

The following morning, Patterson entered his office to find Vera Cross laying out his mail.

Until 04.00, Patterson had tossed and turned in bed, thinking about what Sheila had told him and wondering if it were true, then in desperation, knowing he wouldn't sleep without a pill, he took two and overslept. There was such a scramble to get to the bank in time that he threw on the clothes he had worn the previous night, not caring if the bank raised eyebrows that he was in week-end clothes. In spite of doing without his morning coffee and driving too fast, he was still ten minutes late when he hurried into his offce.

'Oh! Oh!' Vera said softly. 'Someone's had a thick week-end.'

Patterson was in no mood for Vera's good natured banter.

'Let's cut the cackle,' he said curtly and sat down behind his desk. 'I'm late ... okay ... so now ... what's important?'

Startled by his tone, Vera patted the right hand pile of mail. 'There are the men. Would you like me to cope with the boys?'

'Do that.' Patterson lit a cigarette with an unsteady hand, 'And get me a cup of coffee, please. Have I any appointments?'

'Mr Cohen at ten. Mrs Lampson at eleven-fifteen,' Vera said. 'There's no Board meeting.'

'I know that!' he snapped. 'There never is on Monday!'

Behind his back, Vera rolled her eyes. Someone must have soured him, she thought. Yet he looked as if he had had it off. Men! She shrugged.

'Yes, Mr Patterson, sir,' she said.

'And cut that out!' Patterson barked. 'It's not funny!'

She was glad to leave the office.

Patterson rubbed his hand over his badly shaven jaw. He looked across the office at the wall mirror and grimaced. God! He looked a mess! He was thankful he didn't have to attend a Board meeting. He looked at the pile of mail and cursed under his breath. What a life to lead! he thought. He was nothing but a goddamn slave! Such a thought would never have entered his head had he not been obsessed by the thought of an income of one hundred thousand dollars a year.

He stubbed out his cigarette. He immediately wanted another and put his hand in his pocket. He found the box Sheila had given him.

When she had left the previous evening, he had opened the box. In the dim light, he had peered at what seemed to him to be a black button. Obviously it was of no value nor of import-ance and his thoughts were so busy, he had shrugged and drop-ped the box back into his pocket. Now he opened the box and this time regarded the black button more closely: to him, it was still a black button. He took it from the box and found the back was sticky with some powerful adhesive. What the hell was this? he wondered irritably, then as Vera came in with a cup of coffee, he put the button down on his desk and forgot it.

After drinking the coffee, he became more relaxed. He settled down to dictate. In under an hour, he had cleared the mail. When Vera had gone he leaned back in his chair and stared at his blotter. If the old lady had really left him this income for life, he could make plans. She was seventy-eight. She could last for another ten years of course, but that was unlikely. Suppose she lasted another six years: by then he would be thirty-nine. How many men could give up work and retire with one hundred thousand dollars a year? Six years wasn't so long to wait. He took out his handkerchief and wiped his sweating hands. If only he knew for certain!

The only way he could be certain was to read the will. Was this impossible? He sat, thinking. He knew the form. The Legal department, run by Irving Fellows, wouldn't part with the will without authorization from Mrs Morely-Johnson. Would that be so difficult to get? He lit a cigarette, got to his feet and began to pace around his office.

The old lady was half blind. She signed any paper he put before her. He could include an authorization along with Stock transfers. He felt sure she would sign it.

Fellows?

Patterson returned to his desk and sat down.

Fellows was tricky, but if Patterson told him the old lady wanted to review her will and here was the authorization, how could he object?

Again Patterson wiped his hands with his handkerchief. But if he slipped up! If the old lady wanted to know what she was signing! He could have an answer ready ... he would have to have an answer ready! This didn't present a problem, but suppose Fellows telephoned her to check that she wanted to see her will ... the sonofabitch was so tricky he might do just that to curry favour. If that happened, then there would be an inquiry. Patterson flinched at the thought. No job ... no one hundred thousand dollars a year for life!

Patterson, thinking about this, lost his nerve. No! Wait! he told himself. He was young. Don't do anything stupid or dangerous. When working in a bank, you don't do stupid things. One slip ... and you were out!

And yet, he tormented himself, why couldn't he know for certain? To have this hanging over his head until the old lady died! It might be ten years. Goddamn it! She might even outlive him!

There came a tap on the door and Vera looked in.

'Mr Cohen,' she said.

Patterson dragged his mind back to realities and got to his feet.

Bernie Cohen owned a flourishing self-service store, an Amusement Park and a water ski-ing school He always had spare cash and was always looking for a quick turnover. The bulk of his money was safe in high yielding bonds, but with his spare cash, he liked to gamble for capital growth.

Cohen was short, fat, balding, blue-jowled and always smiling. He dwelt behind a six-inch cigar and he had been heard to say: 'If the greatest man of this century smoked cigars, why shouldn't I?' and he would give the V sign with his stubby fat fingers and grin.

Cohen sank into the client's chair and stared at Patterson.

'Moses and Jacob!' he exclaimed. 'Have you had a week-end! What did she do to you?'

Patterson was in no mood to take a ribbing from Cohen.

'What's your problem, Bernie?' he asked, a snap in his voice. 'I have a load of work, so let's get down to it.'

Cohen removed his cigar from his mouth, regarded the cigar, then leaning forward, he knocked the ash into the ash-tray.

'Like that, huh? Sore? That happened to me ... once it was really bad ... a Jap. Brother! Talk about getting caught in a vice.'

'What's your problem?' Patterson said, picking up his gold pencil.

Cohen grimaced.

'You're in a hell of a mood, aren't you, Chris?'

'I'm okay ... what's the problem?'

Cohen hesitated, then he lifted his fat shoulders. If it was going to be only business ... then it was going to be only business.

'How do you like Auto. Cap. Comp?'

Patterson didn't hesitate. He shook his head.

'Not for you ... too long term. Unless you've changed your thinking, you want something quick ... or am I wrong?'

'You're right.'

'How much?'

'Fifty big ones.'

Patterson thought for a moment. He envied Cohen. This fat, ball of a man could afford to gamble. If he won, he smiled. If he lost, he still smiled. Thinking back on their association, Patterson couldn't remember when Cohen had lost ... he had gambler's luck.

'Ferronite,' he said. 'It stands now at $21. There's a hint of a take over. Could go to $29 ... might go higher. It's a quick in and out.'

Cohen grinned.

'That's what my Jap said to me, but she was fooling.'

Patterson put down his gold pencil with an irritable movement that told Cohen this kind of talk wasn't with him this morning.

'Mrs Moses!' Cohen was now worried. 'You're in a hell of a mood, Chris?'

'I have a load of work, Bernie,' Patterson said. 'How about Ferronite?'

Cohen felt deflated. Up to now, he always had enjoyed his sessions with Patterson. They kidded each other, swopped raw jokes, but this morning, Patterson was acting like the goddamn manager of the bank.

'Well, okay ... you say it ... I buy it. Sure go ahead.'

'Fifty thousand?'

'Yes.'

Patterson made a quick note on his pad.

'Fine, Bernie.' He got to his feet. 'Let's have dinner together. How are you fixed ... Friday any good to you?'

Cohen began to smile again.

'Yeah ... will you lay on the girls or shall I?'

Patterson only half heard this. He was again thinking of Mrs Morely-Johnson.

'Hey! How about the girls?' Cohen asked, raising his voice.

Patterson dragged his mind back and shrugged.

'You fix them, Bernie.'

Cohen got to his feet.

'How that chick must have screwed you! Look, I'll call you. You're not in the mood right now. I know how it is. A good ...' He broke off and his smile vanished. 'What's this? What are you playing at?'

The sudden snap in his voice startled Patterson. He stared at Cohen.

'What is what? What do you mean?'

'What's the big idea – bugging me?' Cohen demanded and he pointed to the desk.

Patterson followed the direction of the fat finger and saw Cohen was pointing at the black button Sheila had given him.

'Bugging you?' he said blankly, then as Cohen pulled the button off the desk, he felt a cold sensation move over his body.

'That's what I said. Why are you bugging me?'

'But I'm not! I don't understand what the hell you're talking about!'

'Then why is this on your desk?' Cohen waved the button at Patterson.

'It's a button, isn't it? I – I picked it up in the street ... outside the bank.'

Cohen's little eyes were now like jet beads.

'Do you pick up buttons in the street?'

Stuck with the lie, Patterson said, 'My mother was superstitious. Never pass a button on the street, she used to tell me when I was a kid. Do you walk under a ladder?'

'You really mean to tell me you picked this up on the street?'

'I'm telling you! What the hell is all this, Bernie?'

Cohen suddenly relaxed and he clapped his fat hands down hard on his fat thighs.

'Man! You may be good with money and women, but you're certainly wet behind the ears. You mean you don't know what this is?'

Patterson had a presentiment of disaster, but he managed to keep his face expressionless.

'Should I?'

'This is one of the most sophisticated microphones on the market: a Limpet special. You can stick it anywhere and it can feed a tape recorder a half a mile away: no wires – no nothing. It's one of the most dangerous tools industrial spies are using. Every time I have a board meeting, I have the room checked against this. It's the big ear. You mean you've never seen one before?'

Patterson felt his heart beginning to hammer.

'No.'

'Well, you've seen one now. Get rid of it. Every word we've said could have been taped ... not that it matters.'

Patterson looked so shaken and white that Cohen felt he would be doing him a kindness by leaving.

'Well, so long, Chris ... see you Friday.'

'Yes.'

Cohen paused at the door.

'Mothers are the salt of the earth, but I'd skip picking up buttons if I were you in the future.'

He went out, closing the door behind him.

Five

Patterson got through the rest of the morning only by sheer will power and by forcing his mind to work. He needed to think about the microphone, but that was impossible with continuous telephone calls, Vera popping in and out with papers for him to sign and then Mrs Lampson bleating about her investments, but finally, lunch time arrived and he could escape from the bank.

He drove in the Wildcat to the end of Seaview boulevard to a small restaurant he knew was busy at night, but quiet during the day. He picked a corner table and ordered a whisky on the rocks and a beef sandwich. There were only five other people in the restaurant and they were sitting well away from him.

Now he began to think, and as he thought, a Siberian wind blew through his mind. He knew for certain that he had got himself into a trap. No woman gives her lover a highly sensitive microphone after making love unless this gift was the opening gambit to blackmail.

Patterson was no fool. He was certain all he and she had said in the motel bedroom was now on tape. She had given him the microphone to tell him just this. So now, he asked himself, how was she going to use the tape? How would the approach to blackmail begin? How much was she going to ask?

The whisky helped to steady his nerves. He thought back on the conversation they had had. She had been clever. He had put his signature to the tape. *I, Christopher Patterson, thinks Sheila Oldhill* ... Yes, that had been clever and ruthless. Then she had encouraged him to talk about Mrs Morely-Johnson.

If that tape got into the old lady's hands, he would be finished: not only with her, but also with the bank. She was their most important customer. No woman could stomach what he had said about her in that motel bedroom and not come after his blood.

When the crunch came, would he submit to blackmail? If he could buy back the tape and be sure there wasn't a copy, he would do it, but he was sure there would be a copy.

He finished the whisky and ignored the sandwich.

But Sheila, he told himself, must know he hadn't much money. What could she hope to bleed him for – five thousand dollars? Maybe so much a month? Then he remembered she had told him the old lady was leaving him one hundred thousand dollars a year for life. He was sure now that the old lady hadn't told Sheila this. She must have found out – if she had found it out – by going through the old lady's papers when the old lady was out. She would see her chance of tapping a gold mine. He shook his head. No, he was thinking along the wrong lines because the money only came to him when the old lady was dead and once dead the tape would have no blackmailing power. No, it couldn't be that. It must be a deeper and more cunning motive behind this.

He lit a cigarette as he thought.

Finally, he decided whatever the risk, he had to see Mrs Morely-Johnson's will. That would give him a clue to Sheila's thinking. If he really was to inherit this big income then he would know what to expect when she put the bite on him. He realized, if the money was to come to him and he told Sheila to go to hell, he would not only lose his job at the bank, but Mrs Morely-Johnson would certainly cut him out of her will. The Siberian wind blew even harder as he realized this fact. It might be the only solution to pay blackmail money, but if only he knew for sure he was going to inherit from the old lady. He had to know!

Back at the bank, a half an hour later, he went to his office, took from his desk drawer a sheet of the Plaza Beach Hotel notepaper he kept handy on which to write letters for the old lady to sign. Using his portable typewriter, he wrote the following:

Dear Mr Patterson,
   I am so forgetful these days, I can't remember certain bequests I think I have made in my will. Would you please bring my will at your earliest convenience? It is, I believe, in an envelope in the bank.
   Looking forward to seeing you.

He dated the letter, studied it, decided it was the sort of letter the old lady would write and wouldn't arouse Fellows' suspicions. He then went to his filing cabinet and took out Mrs Morely-Johnson's portfolio.

It took him some twenty minutes to assemble papers for her signature. He placed the letter among these papers and then put them into his brief-case. Then he called the Plaza Beach Hotel.

The operator connected him with the penthouse suite and Sheila answered. The sound of her quiet, calm voice sent a chill through him, but he forced his voice to sound normal.

'This is Chris Patterson. Good afternoon, Miss Oldhill. Would you please ask Mrs Morely-Johnson if I could see her for five minutes in about half an hour? I have papers for her to sign.'

'Will you hold a moment, Mr Patterson?' Her voice was deadpan and impersonal.

There was a delay, then Sheila said, 'Mrs Morely-Johnson will be going out at half past four. If you can come right away...'

'I'll do that,' Patterson said and hung up.

He paused, staring down at his blotter, his heart beating unevenly. Well, he was committed. He had to know. With this threat of blackmail hanging over him, the risk had to be taken. He had to know!

Twenty minutes later, he was ringing on the bell of the penthouse. Sheila opened the door. He stood for a moment, looking at her. He had himself under control and his warm, charming smile appeared as sincere and as genuine as it had always done. He regarded the calm, remote face, the glasses and the low-dressed hair. Neither she nor he let the mask slip.

Sheila stood aside.

'Please come in, Mr Patterson. Mrs Morely-Johnson is on the terrace. She's expecting you.'

Was this really the woman who had writhed so erotically under him not fifteen hours ago? Patterson thought as he walked into the vestibule, All right, you bitch, you can act ... and so can I!

'Thank you. Is Mrs Morely-Johnson well?'

'Yes,' Sheila didn't look at him. 'You know the way ... please go ahead,' and she turned and went into her office.

Patterson stared after her, seeing the long, straight back, the curve of the buttocks and the long legs, remembering how those long legs had twined his body while he had gripped those sleek buttocks.

He walked through the big living-room and out on to the terrace.

'You naughty boy!' Mrs Morely-Johnson exclaimed, obviously delighted to see him. 'You're always worrying me to sign some tiresome paper. Come and sit down.'

He sat beside her, then he stiffened and his body turned cold.

By her was a terrace table and on the table stood a tape recorder.

Patterson stared at the recorder as if he was staring at a coiled snake. His mouth turned dry.

'You're looking at my new toy,' Mrs Morely-Johnson said. 'I'm utterly thrilled with it. I can't think why I never thought of buying one before. It was Sheila's idea. She said I should never play the piano without recording what I play. She said the tapes would go down to posterity ... now isn't that the sweetest thing to say? It's given me so much interest. Just listen to this,' and putting her beautiful, long finger on the play-back button, she pushed it down.

By the time the Chopin Etude had been played, Patterson had absorbed the shock of the tape recorder.

My God! he thought. This bitch is smart. What a sucker punch! First the microphone ... now the tape recorder. She is spelling it out in capital letters!

'There are six tiresome papers for you to sign, then I must run,' he said after praising the old lady's playing. He produced his gold pen, folded back the papers, leaving space only for her signature and handed her the pen.

'What are these papers, Chris?' she asked, fumbling for her glasses.

'They are stock transfers,' Patterson told her. 'I'm sorry to bother you with this, but I'm moving your holdings about quite a bit. You have a profit this month of forty thousand dollars. The market is tricky: you have to buy, then sell and take your profit.'

She had her glasses on now.

'Forty thousand dollars!' She beamed at him. 'You are a clever boy!' She put her dry, hot hand on his. 'And you are very kind.'

'It's my pleasure.' Patterson felt a trickle of sweat run down his face. 'Just here ...'

She signed with her sprawling, almost sightless signature. He turned another page and she signed again. He turned another page, his mouth turning dry, knowing the next page was the letter and not a transfer. Would she spot the difference? Briskly, he turned the page and he stiffened as he saw her pause.

'What's this, Chris?'

He was prepared for this.

'You need a renewal order on the bank for the penthouse rent,' he said. 'This takes care of it.'

'Do I?' She looked up and peered at him. 'I thought ...'

'The bank needs it ... I'm sorry to bother you ...'

'Don't be sorry, Chris. I'm so grateful for your help.'

He watched her scrawl her signature, then he turned to the next page.

Well, it had worked, he thought, drawing in a deep breath. Now, he had to convince Fellows.

The signing over, Mrs Morely-Johnson talked for a while as she held on to Patterson's wrist with her old, dry hand. Patterson listened, smiled, said the right things and wondered when he could escape.

Then Bromhead came out on to the terrace.

'You have ten minutes, ma'am,' he said with a little bow.

'You see?' Mrs Morely-Johnson tapped Patterson playfully on his arm. 'I'm never left in peace. Dine with me tomorrow night at eight o'clock. I will be having a few friends.'

'Thank you ... it will be my pleasure.' Patterson gathered up his papers and put them in his brief-case.

'Black tie, Chris,' she reminded him as he kissed her hand.

He nodded to Bromhead who inclined his head, then let himself out of the penthouse, thankful Sheila remained in her office.

He drove back to the bank. Then steeling himself, and armed with the letter, he went to the Legal department.

Luck was running his way. Irving Fellows had just left in a hurry as he had had news that his eldest son had fallen out of a tree and had broken his arm. Fellows' secretary, a plain, fat woman who thought Patterson was the nearest thing to a movie star, gave him the sealed envelope containing Mrs Morely-Johnson's will in exchange for Mrs Morely-Johnson's authorization.

It was as easy as that.

Gerald Hammett lay on his bed listening to the strident noises coming from the waterfront, to the car horns as the traffic got snarled up and to the chattering voices of the tarts as they came out of the rooming house across the way to begin the afternoon's stint.

He felt lonely and utterly bored and sick of this thing he had agreed to do. If it wasn't for Sheila he would have got on a bus and gone down to Miami. He had never known a woman like Sheila. All the women he had gone with had been hard and tough and had treated him the way a tart treats any man. But Sheila was different. She was the first woman he now could call his own. She was tricky, of course, but he had come to accept all women could be tricky. There were times when she was contemptuous of him. This he accepted as he was contemptuous of himself. If he was asked why this calm, remote woman, several years older than himself, should have had such a hold on him, he would have been hard pressed to explain. The ultimate thing, he thought, was that when they were together in bed, she gave herself in such a way that he knew he owned her and he had never felt that way with any other woman. Once it was over, she became remote again, but that didn't worry him. He knew once she was in the mood, he would get her back. She was exciting to him. She was to him like rolling dice. You never knew what would come up and this way of life was important to him. He hated routine. He wanted his life to be uncertain. He didn't want to wake up tomorrow and do something he had done the day before. Sheila was this kind of woman: they could wake up and she was remote: they could wake up and she was biting his shoulders, her finger-nails clawing his back and there was this explosion that no other woman could ever or would ever give him.

He hated the thought that this handsome banker should be having it off with her. The thought tormented him. He was uneasy that money apparently meant so much to her. He wished now he had never met Bromhead: never agreed to the plan. Until Bromhead had arrived on the scene, Sheila was his whenever he wanted her: they had even been happy together. Then Bromhead had arrived and the scene changed.

Suppose this plan of Bromhead's worked? he thought, staring up at the dirty ceiling. What would he do with all the money Bromhead had said would come to him? He didn't want it! All he really wanted was Sheila, food, a couple of rooms and a car – not even a good car. It was more fun to have a wreck of a car. To go to your car, get in and start it, knowing it would start and go was a drag. The fun with a car was not to know if it would start ... to curse and kick it, to dig into its guts and finally persuade it to start: that was the kind of car he liked. But with all this goddamn money Bromhead had promised him, he knew Sheila would insist that he had a reliable car, good meals, clean sheets, a clean shirt every day ... things he despised.

How sick he was of this luxurious, stinking town. There was nothing to do except spend money. You couldn't move without spending money. Well, he had turned bitchy! He rubbed his sweating face and grinned. He had told Sheila she was to see him every night or he would quit. For once, he had seen something that could be worry come into her smoky blue eyes.

'You come here every night or I'll quit,' he said to her. 'And wear that wig ... I dig for it. If you don't come, I'm taking off. I'm sick of this. Every night or I quit!'

He felt safe talking to her this way. They were now hooked together and without him, she and Bromhead were sunk. For the first time since he had met her, he felt really safe to make demands on her. He was prepared to put up with the boredom of this stinking town only if he saw her every night.

He looked at his cheap wrist-watch. The time was 16.40. At this time Bromhead was driving Mrs Morely-Johnson in the Rolls to a bridge party. Mrs Morely-Johnson's bridge was always painful as she could scarcely see the cards, but her friends were patient and waited while she peered at the cards. Once she knew what she had in her hand she was as good as any of them. Patterson was leaving the bank with Mrs Morely-Johnsons' will in his brief-case. Sheila was using the tape recorder, listening to Patterson's voice. *I, Christopher Patterson ...* and as she listened, her smoky, remote blue eyes lit up, knowing she was listening to a golden voice that could give her what she wanted.

There came a gentle tap on the door and Gerald frowned. Who could this be? he wondered. Not Sheila ... it was too early. He didn't give a damn about anyone else so he remained quiet. The tap came again. Still he remained quiet. He saw the door handle turn and he grinned. He always kept the door locked. He watched the door handle turn full circle and then return. Again the tap came on the door. Gerald waited. Whoever it was would go away. The only person he wanted to see was Sheila and by now, she would have called out. Then he heard a scatching sound which made him sit up, resting himself on his elbow. Then before he could get off the bed, the door opened and a man slid into the room, immediately closing the door.

This man was a mountain of black flesh and muscle. He was the biggest Negro Gerald had ever seen. He filled the small, hot room and his smile, gentle and wide, revealed teeth like piano keys. He wore a plum-coloured turtle-neck sweater and black hipsters. His high-domed head was shaved. His bloodshot, black eyes moved restlessly from side to side. There was a knife scar running down the right side of his face from his ear to his chin: a ridge like a mountain chain on a relief map.

Gerald stared at him. The wide, gentle smile scared him more than if this huge ape had glared at him.

'You're in the wrong room,' Gerald said, not moving. 'Get out!'

The Negro continued to smile and he moved forward so he was standing by the bed, towering over Gerald who stared at him.

'Come on, baby, you and me are travelling,' he said. For a man of his size, his voice was high-pitched and soft. 'Not much time, baby. The bus leaves in half an hour.'

'You heard me ... get out!' Gerald swung his legs to the floor. 'Get out ... nigger!'

Something exploded inside his head. He didn't even see the slap coming. He found himself flat on his back across the bed, dazed, with blinding lights flashing before his eyes, then he realized this monster of a man had cuffed him ... not hit him, but just slapped him. Fury boiled up in him. He was not without courage. No one had ever hit him before and he wanted to hit back. He struggled off the bed and again found himself flat across the bed. The raging pain in his head turned him sick.

'Come on, baby, you and me are travelling. Pack ... the bus goes in half an hour,' the Negro said gently.

Gerald shook his head, trying to get rid of the dancing lights. He began to heave himself off the bed, then a black dry hand closed over his face and slammed him flat.

'Look, baby ... see what I've got for you.'

Gerald stared up at the enormous black fist held close to his eyes. Each finger, looking like a black banana, carried a ring and on each ring was fixed a sharp, cruel spike.

'If I hit you, baby, in your generating system with this, you'll be singing alto in the choir.' The Negro smiled. 'Do you want to sing alto in the choir, baby?'

Gerald cringed away. He had never seen such a terrible weapon and looking up into the black eyes, at the gleaming white teeth and at the scar, he knew this was no bluff and he also knew one violent punch with this spiked horror would emasculate him.

His fury and courage drained out of him.

'What do you want me to do?' he asked, his voice trembling.

'Pack, baby. You and me are travelling.'

Gerald, in spite of his terror, thought of Sheila.

'Where are we going?'

'L.A., baby. You and me are going to have a fine time. You've nothing to worry about ... everything paid. I'm going to be your friend.' The Negro widened his smile. 'I'm Hank Washington ... you call me Hank ... I call you Gerry ... okay, baby?'

His face still aching, sick fear making him tremble, Gerald began to pack. He had few things and the packing was done in minutes. The Negro picked up the battered suitcase.

'You see?' he said, smiling his gentle smile. 'I carry your bag. You and me are friends ... you call me Hank ... I call you Gerry.'

Gerald flinched. He saw the rings on the Negro's hand had disappeared. He wondered if he should make a run for it and the Negro, watching him, seemed to know what was going on in his mind.

'Look, baby, don't let's have any trouble. I've got something else.' He put his hand inside his jacket and a long stabbing knife appeared in his black hand. The thin, menacing blade glittered. 'Baby, I'm a real artist with this sticker.' The knife disappeared. 'It's all going to be fine. Nothing to worry about ... just don't make trouble. Me and trouble never get along together. You make trouble ... you sing alto ... you go along with me ... you have a fine time ... okay, baby?'

'Yes,' Gerald said huskily and followed the Negro out of the room.

The telephone bell rang in Bromhead's room and he lifted the receiver.

'Jack?'

He recognized Solly Marks's wheezing voice.

'That's me.'

'Your problem's taken care of.'

'Thanks.' Bromhead replaced the receiver. He sat for a long moment, thinking. It had to be done. Gerald was becoming a nuisance, but Bromhead now thought uneasily how much his operation was costing him. Solly Marks had agreed to take care of Gerald, have him under constant supervision, feed him and keep him occupied for the sum of ten thousand dollars. Marks didn't seem to operate under a fee of ten thousand dollars. Bromhead had signed yet another I.O.U., knowing he was in the red with Marks for $22,000. He also knew that Marks didn't lend money unless he was certain of collecting. This operation had to succeed!

He continued to think. It looked set, but there could be snags.

Things happened that you didn't think of or couldn't foresee, but the overall plan was working well. He had listened to the tape Sheila had played on the old lady's recorder. What an artist Sheila was! If he had written the script for her, he couldn't have done better. And this inspiration of buying the tape recorder for the old lady! This was something he wouldn't have thought of. How this must have shaken Patterson when he had seen it! He was sure he had Patterson now where he wanted him. Now thanks to Solly Marks, Gerald had been removed from the scene and would be kept on ice until the time was ready to use him. Yes ... the operation was going well!

He got to his feet and left his room. The time was 19.10. Mrs Morely-Johnson would be having cocktails with friends on the terrace. He entered the hotel lobby and crossing to one of the telephone booths, he called the penthouse. Sheila answered.

'Jack,' Bromhead said.

'Come up,' she replied and replaced the receiver.

Bromhead nodded approvingly. No words wasted ... like him ... a professional.

He walked into her office, hearing the chatter of people on the terrace, sure it was safe for them to talk for at least half an hour.

'He's gone to L.A.,' Bromhead said, standing by her desk. 'You don't have to worry about him now.'

Sheila stiffened.

'Gerry's gone? What happened?'

'Don't let's waste time ... he's gone and he's safe. You must now talk to Patterson.'

'I can't believe it! You really mean Gerry's gone?'

'Stop worrying about him ... he's gone.'

She drew in a long breath. Perhaps for the first time, she really realized she was dealing with a man who would let nothing stand between himself and money. She thought of Gerald. He wouldn't have gone unless he had been under some kind of pressure. She looked at Bromhead who was regarding her thoughtfully. She got no clue from his expression as to what had happened.

'Patterson ...' Bromhead said quietly.

'Yes.' She tried to dismiss a frightened Gerald from her mind.

'Don't worry about Patterson,' Bromhead said. 'He's hooked. I bet by now he will have read the will. I don't have to tell you what to do?'

'No.'

'He is having dinner with the old lady tomorrow. You'd better contact him. After dinner, he can come up to the 19th floor and you can have him in your bedroom to talk.'

'Yes.' She thought for a moment, then picked up the telephone receiver and dialled Patterson's home number. The call was immediately answered.

'Chris?'

'Oh ... Sheila! I was expecting to hear from you.' Patterson's voice sounded bland.

'You will be dining with Mrs Morely-Johnson tomorrow evening,' Sheila said. 'When it is over, come to the 19th floor and walk up to the fire door on the 20th floor. You will find it open. I will be waiting for you.'

'I'll do just that, Mata Hari,' Patterson said and hung up.

Sheila looked at Bromhead.

'He could be difficult.'

Bromhead shook his head.

'No one is ever difficult when he wants money,' he said. 'Don't worry.'

Abe Weidman, short, thickset, balding, walked with Patterson across the lobby of the hotel to the exit. The two men had been in the bar for a nightcap. As Mrs Morely-Johnson's attorney, Weidman imagined he and she were the only people to know that the old lady was leaving Patterson one hundred thousand dollars a year for life. He now regarded Patterson as one of his important people: a future client. He also liked this handsome man and he conveyed this by holding Patterson's arm as they walked across the soft pile of the carpet to the revolving doors.

'An excellent dinner,' he said. 'A first-class claret. The old lady still knows how to entertain.'

'Yes,' Patterson said. In a few minutes, he was thinking, he would have to face Sheila. His mind was excited. He had read the will and knew for certain that he was to inherit this big income. But he had still to cope with Sheila. It needed will power to appear relaxed and interested as he walked by Weidman's side.

'She looks well,' Weidman said, pausing at the top of the steps. 'Of course, none of us are getting any younger. Still, she could last for years. Can I give you a lift?'

'Thanks ... no. I have a telephone call to make.'

'You bankers ...' Weidman patted Patterson's arm. 'You're always busy.'

Patterson laughed.

'You know how it is.'

Weidman clasped his hand.

'Have lunch with me next week. I'll get my girl to call your girl.'

'Sure. I'd like that ... thanks.'

Weidman waved his cigar.

'Then next week.'

Patterson watched him walk heavily down to his glittering Cadillac. As the chauffeur held open the door, Weidman turned and waved again and Patterson waved back. He knew Weidman knew and this was the reason why he had been invited to lunch. Weidman was looking ahead: a future client. Well, it wasn't in the bag yet, Patterson thought as he recrossed the lobby and entered the elevator which was now on automatic. He felt it was now safe to go up: the old lady would be in bed.

Joe Handley, the hotel detective, was in the lobby. He watched Patterson enter the elevator and decided Patterson who he knew had been dining with Mrs Morely-Johnson, had forgotten something. He watched the indicator as it moved swiftly from floor to floor, then when it stopped at the 19th floor, Handley frowned. Why had Patterson got out on the 19th floor he asked himself. Handley kept a notebook in which he jotted unusual happenings that seemed to be of importance. There could be, of course, a straight forward explanation, but this puzzled him. None of the four old couples, living on the 19th floor, were likely to want to see an assistant bank manager at 22.15. Then remembering Lawson's warning not to stick his nose into Mrs Morely-Johnson's guests' affairs, he made a note in his book and left it like that.

As the elevator took Patterson, swiftly and smoothly, up to the 19th floor, he tried to relax. He knew for certain the dice was loaded against him. If he hadn't walked into Sheila's trap, he could be confident that when Mrs Morely-Johnson died, he would be a wealthy man for life, but he had walked into the trap and now he had to negotiate. He was worth around thirty thousand dollars. At a pinch, he could pay Sheila fifteen hundred dollars a month out of his salary. But would she be content with that? He doubted it, but it was no use speculating until he had talked to her. She might have completely different ideas, but whatever her ideas, he had made up his mind, even if he had to pay outrageous blackmail, he would try to hang on to Mrs Morely-Johnson's legacy.

Arriving at the 19th floor, he walked up the stairs facing him to find the fire door standing ajar. He moved into Sheila's bedroom and closed the door.

Sheila was sitting in a small lounging chair, an open book on her lap. She was wearing a white blouse and a black skirt: the same clothes she had worn when receiving Mrs Morely-Johnson's guests.

'Thank you for coming,' she said, her voice low. 'Sit down.'

Patterson sat in the other lounging chair, facing her and regarded her. Her calm expression and her remote, smoky blue eyes bothered him. He remembered the woman clawing at him and gasping as he had thrust into her. She was an enigma to him and enigmas worried him.

'You have read the will?' she asked.

'I've read it.'

'Good. Then you know now I've been telling the truth.'

'Yes.'

'Do you want all this money?'

They stared at each other. Both kept their faces expressionless.

'I want it,' Patterson said.

'You would be stupid if you didn't. Are you prepared to earn it?'

Here it comes, Patterson though. God! She's a professional! Not one word wasted.

'That depends,' he said.

There was a long pause as she regarded him.

'Depends on ... what?'

He resisted the urge to uncross and recross his legs. He forced himself to appear relaxed.

'On the conditions, of course,' he said and smiled at her. 'You do realize this is blackmail, don't you? You can go to jail for quite a while for blackmail.'

She nodded.

'Yes ... I know.' She waved to the telephone standing on the bedside table. 'Call the police ... tell them.'

Again they stared at each other.

'You're quite a woman,' Patterson said. 'Okay, so what are the conditions?'

'You have the will?'

'Yes ... it goes back to our legal department tomorrow.'

'I want it.'

This startled him and he stared at her.

'You want her will? What use is it to you?'

She opened a box by her side and took out a cigarette. Patterson left his chair to light the cigarette. Her soft, warm fingers touched his and he felt a stab of desire go through him. He returned to his chair and again they looked at each other.

'Would you like to hear the tape?' she asked. 'I've borrowed the recorder.'

Patterson, uneasy that simply by touching her hand, his blood had become on fire, shook his head.

'I can imagine.' He pulled himself together. 'Let's get this right. The theory is if I don't do what you want – whatever it is you want – you play the tape to the old lady and I lose my job at the bank and get cut out of the will ... that's it, isn't it?'

She nodded.

'Yes.'

His mind working swiftly, Patterson asked, 'You want the will ... and what else?'

'Will you give me the will?'

'I could do. Look, Sheila, you have me in a trap. I admit it. I want the old lady's money. I admit that. It could change my life. I'm ready to go along with you because I have to. Wouldn't it be better for both of us if you put your cards on the table and told me just what this is all about?'

As Sheila hesitated, the fire door opened and Bromhead came in. He was wearing a charcoal grey suit, a white shirt and a grey tie. He looked like a bishop attending a committee meeting.

Patterson stared at him. His quick mind immediately saw the connection between these two. Even as Bromhead quietly closed the door, Patterson had recovered from the shock.

'Perhaps I had better explain,' Bromhead said, looking at Sheila. 'We must take Mr Patterson into our confidence.'

'Yes.' Sheila relaxed back in her chair.

Bromhead came further into the room and moving around Patterson, he sat on the bed.

'You ask us to put our cards on the table, Mr Patterson,' he said. 'Let me do this. You have read Mrs Morely-Johnson's will. There are several million dollars involved. With your assistance I propose to alter the will so that her nephew receives a million and a half dollars. Your bequest, of course, won't be disturbed. You will still receive one hundred thousand dollars a year for life which represents a considerable capital outlay. But the money is there. You might say, Mr Patterson, that I am acting on behalf of Mrs Morely-Johnson's nephew who has been excluded from the old lady's will. I feel people who give large sums of money to charities, even if they are such worthy charities as the Cancer Research Fund should first consider their relations.'

Listening to the quiet voice, absorbing what he was told, Patterson was also thinking.

'I had no idea the old lady had a nephew,' he said.

'Yes ... she has a nephew: not what you could call a success. He has had trouble with the police. Mrs Morely-Johnson doesn't approve of him. But to me, that is neither here nor there. I like the young man. Sheila likes him. We have decided to help him by rearranging the old lady's will so that he gets a million and a half. It will be arranged with your help in such a way that the old lady won't know.' Bromhead regarded Patterson and he smiled his benign smile. 'I think it would be a fair statement if I said, the dead don't care ... but the living do.'

Patterson considered this, then he nodded.

'Yes. You're not being entirely philanthropic about this?' He regarded Bromhead. 'The nephew won't get all this money?'

'No, Mr Patterson, there will be a division,' Bromhead said in his bishop's voice.

'So what do you expect me to do?'

'You have admitted that if you are unco-operative, you will lose your inheritance,' Bromhead said. 'I don't want you to think I'm bluffing. With so much money involved, bluff is dangerous. Would you be patient please? I think you should hear the quality of the tape we have.' He looked at Sheila. 'Would you please?'

Sheila leaned down. The tape recorder was on the floor out of sight by her chair. She pressed the play-back button.

Patterson heard his voice saying: *I, Christopher Patterson thinks Sheila Oldhill* ... and so on. Then he listened to the real damning thing he had said: *Do you want me to spell it out? At the age of seventy-eight, she is vain, half blind, gushing and she can't keep her eyes off young men.*

He listened to the rest of the tape with indifference. He was trapped and he knew it. If the old lady ever heard this ... no job ... no one hundred thousand dollars a year for life.

'It's impressive, isn't it?' Bromhead said quietly. 'A nice recording. I have a copy of course.'

Patterson produced his gold cigarette case, selected a cigarette and lit it with his gold lighter.

'I asked you what you expected me to do?'

'First, I want the will.'

'You can have it, but I don't see what good it will do you. You're not telling me you hope to forge her signature, are you?'

Bromhead nodded.

'That's what I intend to do.'

'You may think you can,' Patterson said impatiently, 'but Weidman, her attorney, won't be fooled. Weidman and I know her signature backwards. That's something you won't get away with.'

Bromhead took from his hip pocket a scratch pad and he produced a Parker pen.

'Mr Patterson, allow me to give you a little demonstration. Would you sign your name on this pad, please?'

Patterson hesitated, then taking the pad he scrawled his signature and handed back the pad. He watched Bromhead study the signature.

'This is, of course, a little more complicated than Mrs Morely-Johnson's signature,' Bromhead said. 'Still . . .'

He tore off the sheet, then without hesitation reproduced Patterson's signature, shuffled the two pieces of paper quickly and handed them back to Patterson.

'Which is yours?'

Patterson studied the two signatures, then he felt a tingle crawl up his spine. In spite of his years of experience checking signatures while working in the bank, he could not tell which was his signature nor which was the one Bromhead had forged.

'It's an art,' Bromhead said. 'You see that now? You realize now, Mr Patterson, I would have no trouble in reproducing the old lady's signature.' He took up the pad and scrawled, then handed the pad to Patterson. 'I have studied her signature. Look . . .'

Patterson studied the signature, then slowly tore up the three pieces of paper. He put the bits in the ash-tray.

'So . . . you can forge the old lady's signature. I go along with that, but there are the witnesses.'

Bromhead nodded.

'Of course. That has been arranged. I have two witnesses who, for a small sum, if questioned will swear they witnessed the old lady's signature.'

Patterson shook his head.

'No . . . that won't work. Her attorney would never stand for that. No, he would start an inquiry.'

'Mr Patterson, you must give me credit for thinking this out.

You have read the will. You will have seen that Mr Weidman, her attorney, gets nothing. Now, I will arrange it that the old lady has changed her mind. Mr Weidman is going to inherit her three Picasso paintings. I know he wants them. I have often observed him looking at them when calling on the old lady. I can tell by his expression these are really what he covets. It is very simple. She wants to surprise him. So she makes a new will, using a new attorney. She gives her nephew a million and a half dollars and her attorney three Picassos worth maybe five hundred thousand. Do you imagine Mr Weidman would contest such a will?'

Patterson stubbed out his cigarette as he thought.

'So what do you expect me to do?' he asked.

'You will give me the will so I can redraft it, and you will tell Mr Weidman that the old lady has drafted a new will and she has used another attorney because she wants Mr Weidman to be surprised. You will also tell him she has had a change of heart about her nephew and is leaving him a considerable sum. We want Mr Weidman to be prepared and not to make difficulties.'

'You talk as if the old lady is dying,' Patterson said, staring at Bromhead.

'This is a long term operation, Mr Patterson,' Bromhead smiled his benign smile, 'but no one lives for ever.'

'And if I do this,' Patterson said, 'I get the tape?'

'No, you don't get the tape, but you can be sure we won't use it. This is a long-term operation: give me the will, convince Mr Weidman and you can forget the tape. It certainly wouldn't be in our interest to let the old lady hear it . . . you can forget it.'

Patterson lit another cigarette. He was in a trap. If he went to the police he would lose his job and this glittering inheritance. The dead don't care. That was right. Why should he care so long as he got his inheritance? Why should he care if the Cancer Research Fund lost a million and a half dollars?

'Okay,' he said, getting to his feet. 'I'll talk to Mr Weidman. I'll leave the will in a sealed envelope addressed to Miss Oldhill with the hall porter.'

'Thank you, Mr Patterson,' Bromhead said.

There was a long pause while Bromhead and Sheila listened as the elevator descended, then Bromhead smiled.

'You see? It worked. You must never worry.'

'I'll try to remember that.' She got slowly to her feet.

'You're doing very well.' Bromhead crossed to the fire door. 'Think what it will mean to you.'

'Yes.'

When he had gone, Sheila ran off the tape, put it in a box and the box in her bedside table drawer.

She undressed and got into bed. She thought of Gerald. Where was he? What was happening to him? Was someone going around with him, watching him? Once Bromhead had the forged will and lodged it in the bank, then it was just a matter of time. She intended to leave the old lady, find work – a nurse could always find work – and she and Gerald would continue to live as they had done. They would wait until the old lady died. Bromhead had kept saying: No one lives for ever. He had also said it would be a long-term operation. A gamble, Sheila thought. The old lady could die tomorrow or she could live another five years. She flinched. In those five years, Gerald might find someone younger.

It wasn't until the grey light of dawn began to filter through the blinds that she fell asleep.

Lunch at the Lincoln Club was always an event. It was the most expensive and best restaurant in town, and the food was impeccable. Patterson was surprised that Abe Weidman had invited him to such a place. Obviously, he was pulling out all the stops. Patterson had never been to the Lincoln Club before and he was impressed by its massive richness and calm.

He was also impressed that Weidman had his own special table in a far corner in the big crowded restaurant.

'Mr Patterson?' The *maître d'hôtel* had bowed. 'Of course, Mr Weidman is already here at his table. Please, sir ... follow me.'

The *maître d'hôtel* looked like an Ambassador of some rich South American state. He led the way through the tables, his hand up in the air as if he was conducting a train over difficult crossings. Abe Weidman was already sipping a treble gin-martini. He got up and clasped Patterson's hand in his moist warm grip.

A triple gin-martini appeared as if by magic for Patterson and Weidman toasted him.

'Well, Chris, it's good to see you. Let's get the food ordered. The swill here isn't so bad. How about a little smoked salmon and let's split a pheasant between us?'

'Anything you say.' Patterson tried to conceal how impressed he was with Weidman's genuine power. 'Sounds fine to me.'

Weidman looked at the *maître d'hôtel*.

'Then smoked salmon with horse-radish sauce ... some buttered shrimps. How about a pheasant? I won't have it if it hasn't been properly hung ... has it?' The little beady eyes probed.

'It's perfect for you, Mr Weidman.'

'Okay ... all the trimmings. Vodka with the salmon and the Haut Brion with the bird.'

Patterson toyed with his drink, listening. This was a man who was living in a higher bracket than himself, but given time, he would be able to match him. He wondered when he could begin to talk business.

He had seen the forged will. Bromhead had come to his apartment and had given it to him. He had read it through while Bromhead in his role of a servant, had stood respectfully by the door, watching him. He had made sure that his own bequest hadn't been disturbed. The will stated that Mrs Morely-Johnson felt she would like to give her nephew, Gerald Hammett, a second chance. As her only relative, she had decided to give him the sum of one and a half million dollars with which he could do exactly what he liked. The three Picassos, correctly identified, were left to Mr Abe Weidman for services rendered. It was a well constructed document and Patterson could find no flaw in it. The two witnesses of Mrs Morely-Johnson's forged signature were Flo Mackintosh and Hilda Green.

Patterson had queried these two women.

'No trouble,' Bromhead had said. 'They work at the hotel, Mr Patterson. Both of them are thieves. A word from me and they would be in jail ... no trouble.'

When Bromhead had gone, Patterson put the will in an envelope, sealed it, and in the morning had given it to Fellows' secretary. She gave him a receipt to give to Mrs Morely-Johnson and put the envelope in the safe. Back in his office, Patterson had destroyed the receipt. That stage of the operation as far as he was concerned was completed.

Now he had to handle Abe Weidman.

'You know something?' Weidman said as they waited for the smoked salmon to be served. 'You and I could do business together. I have a number of clients who don't know what to do with their money. You know the market and you're smart. Mrs Lampson and that old bitch, Mrs Van Davis – God! That woman gives me ulcers! – both say how smart you are. Come to that, I was talking to Bernie Cohen ... he put in a good word for you.'

'That's fine,' Patterson said. 'I'd be happy to do anything I can, Mr Weidman.'

Weidman waved his fat hand.

'Let's drop the Mister crap ... call me Abe, Chris.'

Patterson turned on his charm.

'Glad to.'

After the smoked salmon had been served and they had sipped their Vodka, Weidman said, 'Strictly between you and me, Chris, the old lady is going to take care of you. This is in strictest confidence, you understand, but a wink is as good as a nod to a blind horse as my old father used to say. I can't tell you more, but you're going to be all right.'

Patterson kept his face expressionless.

'It's good of you, Abe, to tell me this,' he said. 'I had no idea. She's always been kind to me, but ...'

'Put it away in the back of your mind.' Weidman helped himself to horse-radish sauce and then squeezed a lemon over the thick slices of smoked salmon. 'Just thought I would give you a nudge.'

This was the time, Patterson thought. He sat for a moment in silence, then he said, 'I have something to tell you too, Abe, since we are exchanging confidences, but this is really strictly under your hat.'

Weidman looked sharply at him.

'What's that?'

'I could lose my job telling you this, Abe ... it goes no further?'

Startled, Weidman nodded.

'You have my word.'

Patterson appeared to hesitate, then he said, lowering his voice, 'Three days ago, the old lady asked for her will. I gave it to her. She told me she was making changes and she didn't want you to know about it.'

Weidman looked shocked. The smoked salmon on his fork was forgotten.

'You mean she's gone to another attorney?'

'Yes.'

'Jesus! Who?'

'She didn't tell me.'

Blood rushed into Weidman's face, then it receded, leaving him white with anger.'

'Well, for God's sake! How could she do this to me? Has she gone crazy? I've handled her affairs ever since her husband died!'

'Wait a moment, Abe,' Patterson said soothingly. 'When she told me I pointed out how annoyed you would be. I said she was making a mistake ... then because I really scolded her, she told me her reason. I think you should know although I'm betraying a confidence. She wants to surprise you: she's leaving you something in her will.'

Weidman put down his fork. His anger went away and now he looked quizzingly at Patterson.

'She told you that?'

'She had to. I was putting pressure on her. I said she just couldn't go to another attorney.'

Weidman nodded.

'I'll remember that, Chris. So the old girl's leaving me something?'

'Since we are going to work together, Abe, maybe I can give away a confidence. You're getting her three Picassos.'

Weidman stared at him and his little eyes opened wide. He seldom envied people anything but every time he visited the penthouse, he had stared longingly at the three early Picassos in the vestibule. He fancied himself as an amateur collector and he had already some good modern paintings, but no Picassos.

'You really mean that?'

'That was what she told me. She said you would get much more pleasure from them than the local museum.'

'Well!' Weidman couldn't conceal his excitement and happiness. He beamed at Patterson. 'This is wonderful news.'

'She told me something else,' Patterson said, feeling he was now edging out on to thin ice. 'She's changed her mind about her nephew, Gerald Hammett. She's leaving him a hell of a lot of money. She didn't say how much, but I got the impression it was a lot.'

This didn't interest Weidman. He was thinking of the Picassos.

'She is?'

'That's what she told me.'

'Well, good luck to him.' Weidman laid a fat hand on Patterson's arm. 'Sounds like you and me are going to benefit.' He snapped his fingers at the wine waiter. 'This calls for a celebration. We're going to have with our bird, the best claret this swill house has got.'

He ordered a Chateau Margaux 1929 that cost a little over one hundred dollars.

Watching him, seeing the excited expression in the little eyes, Patterson knew there would be no trouble when the will was proved.

Six

Bromhead was watching the late night TV show in his room when the telephone bell rang. He picked up the receiver and as he listened to wheezy breathing, he knew Solly Marks was calling him.

'Jack?'

'That's me,' Bromhead said.

'I'll be at the Franklin at six tomorrow evening,' and the line went dead.

Bromhead replaced the receiver. He got to his feet and turned off the TV set. For a long moment he stood, thinking. This could mean either of two things. It was now three weeks and four days since Gerald had been removed from the scene so either Gerald could be causing trouble or Marks wanted more money.

Suddenly and for the first time, Bromhead felt uneasy. The last thing he wanted was pressure. This was, and had to be, a long term operation, but now he began to realize that circumstances beyond his control could force him to move quicker than was safe.

He wondered if he should consult Sheila but decided this was his own problem. Besides, he didn't entirely trust her where Gerald was concerned. He was sure she would turn difficult if she knew just what was happening to Gerald. There would be time to talk to her when he had seen Marks.

The following evening, he found Marks in the Franklin lobby, smoking a cigar and sipping whisky. The two men shook hands and Bromhead sat beside Marks. At this hour the lobby was deserted. A Negro barman brought Bromhead a whisky on the rocks. When he had gone, Bromhead asked, 'What is it? Trouble?'

'Your problem is acting up.'

Bromhead sipped his whisky.

'I paid you ten thousand to keep him happy.'

'That's correct, but it is now twenty-nine days. That's a long time to keep someone like your problem on ice. Hank is getting tired of it. Two days ago, your problem got away. Hank picked him up at the bus station as he was boarding a bus back here.'

'How did he get away?'

Marks shrugged.

'Hank can't be with him every minute. Hank thinks there should be a second guard. He has a point. Hank has to sleep. Should I get a second guard?'

Bromhead finished his whisky. Here was the bite again. He had smelt it coming. Once committed, you had to pay, he thought wryly, but there would be plenty of money once the operation was completed.

'How much?'

Marks sipped his drink.

'This is getting tricky, Jack. If your problem turns nasty and it looks as if he could, he could have Hank on a snatch rap. I'd say another ten thousand.'

'Can't you think in lesser figures than that?' Bromhead asked, an edge to his voice. 'It's always ten with you.'

Marks stared off into space.

'I said it could turn tricky. You want a good guard, don't you?'

Bromhead knew he was caught. Now the pay-off would be upped to $32,000, but he still could afford that. There would be plenty left for him and Sheila even after paying that amount.

'Yes.' He took out his scratch pad and wrote an I.O.U. for ten thousand dollars and signed it. He handed it to Marks who studied it then looked at Bromhead.

'You've got yourself a big deal then?' he said, showing curiosity for the first time.

'It's big enough,' Bromhead returned, his face wooden.

Marks nodded, then put the I.O.U. in his billfold.

'Okay, Jack, your problem will be taken care of but I must warn you, he doesn't like it. I take no responsibility when we turn him loose. Hank tells me had had to smack him a number of times to keep him in line.'

'Let's cross that bridge when we reach it.'

Marks shrugged.

'It's your bridge ... not mine.'

Bromhead didn't have to be told. He got to his feet.

'Keep him cool for another week. I'll handle him then.'

'How long will it take you to repay me, Jack?' Marks asked, looking up at him.

'I don't know. This operation can't be hurried. You get interest.'

'The interest goes up after three months,' Marks said quietly. 'Forty per cent. Then fifty per cent after the next three months.'

'You look after yourself, don't you?' Bromhead said.

'Yes ... I also have a collecting service.' Marks sipped his drink while he stared at Bromhead. 'I thought I'd remind you.'

'I know,' Bromhead said quietly. 'I've heard about it.'

He had heard about the thugs who collected bad debts for Marks. They arrived with a lead pipe wrapped in a newspaper, made their request politely and then if it wasn't met, turned the client into an idiot by beating him scientifically and repeatedly over the head.

Marks offered his moist, fat hand.

'Just so long as we understand each other, Jack ... it's a lot of money.'

As Bromhead left the Franklin hotel and began to walk along the crowded boulevard towards the Plaza Beach Hotel he knew he would now have to hurry up the operation. The red light was flashing. If only Gerald had been co-operative! Twenty thousand dollars would have been saved. When he had first met him and put up the proposition, he had felt that Gerald could prove tricky, but he had to use him. Sheila had assured him that she could control him. He had been impressed by Sheila. At the time, this seemed to Bromhead to be a fair gamble. When he had conceived the plan, it had seemed simple and straightforward. You found a very rich old woman. (He had done that.) You forged her will. (He had done that.) You arranged to leave a large sum of money to this old woman's nephew. (This too he had done.) You then sat back and waited until the old lady died and then you collected the money. As a theoretical operation it looked good, but now Bromhead wasn't so sure. He realized he hadn't taken into account that there were some people who didn't care about money the way he did. He was getting old, he thought as he walked along the boulevard. He had lost touch with the young: the new generation. When he had been Gerald's age, he would have done anything – repeat anything – to own a million dollars, and yet this dirty, little creep seemed indifferent to money such as this.

Bromhead began to do sums in his head. The take was one and a half million dollars. When the old lady died, this sum would be split up between the three of them, but first, Marks had to be repaid. Give and take, each of them would get just under five hundred thousand. With that kind of money, Bromhead had hoped to give up work, gain security and live decently. Sheila and Gerald would be sitting pretty. They would have a million between the two of them. He would be glad to get rid of them.

But now the operation had become complicated. Marks was threatening him. *Fifty per cent interest after the next three months.* This operation could go on for years. It depended on how long the old lady lived. Would Marks wait years? *I have a collecting service.* Bromhead now realized the weakness of his planning. If Gerald had co-operated he wouldn't be in this financial hole and under pressure with Marks. This had to be thought about. Ahead of him was a café and he went in and sat at a corner table. He asked for a cup of coffee. When the coffee was served, he gave his mind to the problem.

After some five minutes of thought, he came to the reluctant conclusion that with this complication that Gerald had created he could no longer consider this operation as long term. The forged will was back in the bank. If Mrs Morley-Johnson happened to die within the next few weeks, his problems would be solved. Thinking about this, he realized that all the time, at the back of his mind, there had been the possibility of accelerating her death. In fact, the more he thought about it, now the thought was admitted, he saw that to have hoped that this plan could have succeeded by just waiting for her to die was a fantasy.

Bromhead sipped his coffee.

But it was one thing to want the old lady dead and quite something else to arrange her death. He realized she was in an impregnable position; in a penthouse with Sheila always in attendance, guarded by the hall porter and when she went down to the restaurant, she was guarded by bowing waiters. When she went out in the Rolls she was guarded by himself. The one thing he had to be very sure of was not to get himself involved. If the police had any reason to look into his past, he would be a dead duck. He thought of Sheila. She was a trained nurse. Perhaps too many sleeping pills? He toyed with the idea, then shook his head. Sheila was an odd woman, but he had an instinctive feeling she wouldn't touch murder. She wanted money. She was prepared to go along with forgery, but he was certain he couldn't hint at murder to her ... not even hint.

Yet there must be a solution. Success now depended on the old lady dying within a few weeks. He must have nothing to do with her death. Sheila, anyway, would have nothing to do with her death ... then who could he call on to murder the old lady and murder her in such a way that he (Bromhead) and Sheila were without suspicion?

He finished his coffee and lit a cigarette.

Suppose he succeeded in finding someone? To hire someone to kill the old lady was dangerous. There was always the element of blackmail to be considered. But suppose he did find someone he could trust. How would this man get into the penthouse? How would he get by the hall porter and Fred Lawson? What reason could this hired killer give the hall porter to get up to the penthouse? How about Sheila? She would be with the old lady. Bromhead crossed and recrossed his legs as he thought. Suppose he found the solution and got his man up to the penthouse. The killer couldn't just walk in, kill the old lady and walk out again. There had to be an acceptable motive ... but what motive? If the police didn't have a motive to work on, they would dig and this Bromhead knew had to be avoided. He must have a watertight alibi. He would also have to arrange for Sheila to be beyond suspicion.

He relaxed while he thought. Where to find a professional killer? It would be too dangerous to consult Solly Marks. Marks would certainly blackmail him for the rest of his days. He continued to think. Was there someone out of his past he could call on and trust? His mind moved back into the past years ... then he remembered Harry Miller.

Harry Miller!

He thumped his fist into the palm of his hand.

Here was the solution!

He sat thinking, then he got to his feet, paid his check and walked out into the hot night.

If you thought hard enough, he told himself as he walked towards the Plaza Beach Hotel, problems could always be solved, but you had to think and think and think and then remember.

He was whistling softly under his breath, now completely relaxed, as he walked up the steps to the hotel lobby. Making his way to the telephone booths, he found a New York telephone book. He flicked through the pages and finally came to the name:.

Harry Miller

with the address and the telephone number.

He slammed the book shut. It was as if he was slamming the life of Mrs Morely-Johnson's life shut and opening a new life for himself.

On a hot humid morning in New York, a man known as Harry Miller received a bulky envelope: the first letter he had had for many months.

His landlady was so impressed that she climbed the four flights of stairs, panting, to deliver the letter in person. She waited hopefully to see if Harry would give her any information, but Harry took the letter without even a word of thanks and shut his room door in her face.

Harry hated receiving letters. To him, letters always meant trouble, but as this letter had arrived, he opened it. From it spilled an airline ticket, a one-hundred-dollar bill and a note which read:

I need you. I'll be at the airport on 20th. Jack.

Harry frowned as he stared into space.

Jack?

He nodded to himself. Jack ... yes ... Jack Bromhead, the master forger. Harry re-read the note, now interested. It was over five years since he and Bromhead had seen each other. If it hadn't been for Bromhead ...

Although it was five years ago, he remembered exactly what he had said to Bromhead after the event. He had said: *I don't forget. If ever you want me for anything, say so, and I'll pay my debt.*

Oddly enough, considering his character and his viciousness, Harry Miller was a man of his word. So now Bromhead wanted him. Again Harry nodded to himself. That was fine with him. He had had Bromhead on his conscience for five years, wanting to repay him. The only thing that really irked him in this modern world was to be in someone's debt.

His mind moved back into the past. Even now, thinking about it, he flinched. Three of them had ganged up on him. He could have taken two of them, but not the third. It had happened in the prison yard. He had had a suspicion that the word had come into the prison to fix him. He had been serving a five-year stretch for robbery with violence and that had been a mistake. At that time money ran through his fingers like water. He wasn't a stick-up man: he was by profession a killer. He worked for various organizations and he made good money, but at that time, he had a weakness for playing the horses. He had had a good tip that looked certain, but his own trade was slack and he was suddenly without money, so stupidly, he had walked into a gas station, knocked the attendant cold, and as he was rifling the safe, a tough-looking cop had appeared, a ·38 police special in his hairy hand.

The gas attendant had sustained a split skull and the Judge was told that he wouldn't be of much use even though the surgeon had riveted his skull together so Harry was given five years.

Unluckily for him, some months previously he had done a job on a squealer, Toni Bianco. It had been a neat, quick job and Toni had died without knowing he was leaving this life for ever. It so happened that Toni's brother, Luigi, was serving twenty years, for killing a cop, in the prison to which Harry was sent. The word got over the prison walls that Harry was the man who had knocked off Toni Bianco. Luigi felt he had to do something about this but he knew Harry was a button man and he wasn't taking any chances. He found two Italians who agreed to help out. The three of them isolated Harry in a distant corner of the prison yard. They had knives made from roof slates, lovingly filed into needle-like points. As they came at him, Harry realized he could take two of them, but the third one would get him and he began to kiss life goodbye. Then Bromhead appeared. While Harry took care of Luigi and the second man, Bromhead took care of the third man. It was all over in seconds.

Thinking about this, Harry again told himself that if it hadn't been for Bromhead he wouldn't now be breathing nor would his heart be beating. This was a debt that had to be repaid.

I need you.

Harry was pleased. This day was the sixteenth. He had plenty of time. Bromhead was acting big: the air ticket and the one hundred dollar bill. This also pleased Harry. He regarded Bromhead with respect. Bromhead was a craftsman: he could forge any goddamn signature and in a fight he was as good and as tough as Harry himself. So with the air ticket and the money, it looked as if Bromhead was doing well. The hundred dollar bill meant nothing to Harry. Ever since he was released from prison, he had given up playing the horses. During the following five years as a professional killer, he had salted away enough to bring him an invested income, tax free, of around three thousand dollars. Now retired, Harry preferred to live a simple life. His only extravagance was to release a pent-up viciousness every six months by hiring a special whore and thrashing her until the viciousness had drained out of him. Apart from this extravagance, Harry led a quiet life. He liked to watch television, go to the new movies and read books by authors like Harold Robbins. He had no friends . . . friends to him were dangerous and tricky. Friends always wanted something, always vomited out their troubles, always on the scrounge, but never gave anything in return. Long ago, he had learned he could do without friends.

At the age of forty-eight, Harry was under-sized and thin with hollow cheeks, quick steady green eyes, a pinched nose and an almost lipless mouth. He kept himself always in peak condition by morning work-outs with a pair of heavy Indian clubs. He had no more respect for a human life than he had for the life of a fly.

He was a man who killed with his hands. He considered a gun noisy and therefore dangerous, a knife messy and a length of lead piping unprofessional. He had studied the art of karate and he was now an expert. He could smash a brick with the side of either hand with one chopping, terrible blow. The sides of his hands were his weapons: safe and sure. Should some nosy cop stop and frisk him, the cop would never find on him any kind of weapon. The cop wouldn't have the imagination to realize that the sides of Harry's hands were far more lethal than any gun, knife or length of piping.

In his youth, Harry had been bitten by the theatre bug. He had shown a small talent and had acted in various corny plays, playing various corny roles out in the sticks. He had acquired a talent for make-up and this talent he carried into his life of crime. He became known to the F.B.I. and the police as 'the thug with many faces'.

On the twentieth of the month, he arrived at the airport, carrying a small black handbag. He had decided to surprise Bromhead who had said he would be waiting to meet him.

Harry had taken considerable trouble to disguise himself.

Rubber pads against his gums and up his pinched nose had fattened his face. The thick black moustache, each hair carefully and lovingly gummed into place, the black hair which was naturally blond, the horn-rimmed glasses made him someone that Bromhead couldn't possibly recognize.

Bromhead waited at the exit of the arrival centre, his eyes scanning the passengers as they came out. He saw no one remotely resembling Harry Miller. It was only when steel-like fingers closed around his wrist, and a familiar voice said, 'Hi, Jack! Long time no see,' that he realized Harry had arrived.

Twenty minutes later the two men were in the privacy of a motel cabin some two miles from the airport. They talked; or rather Bromhead talked and Harry listened.

For some moments, Harry couldn't believe what Bromhead was telling him.

'Hey, Jack! An old bag of seventy-eight?' He stared at Bromhead. 'You're asking me to knock her off?'

'That's the job, Harry,' Bromhead said. 'It is important to me.'

Harry laughed.

'Well, for Pete's sake! I thought I had something tough. Okay, Jack, boy, I'll take care of it ... just tell me how you want me to handle it.'

Bromhead had been sure this would be the answer, but he was relieved that his thinking had been right.

'I'm not asking you to do this for nothing, Harry,' he said. 'The old lady always wears a mass of jewellery. It's worth something like two hundred grand. There are days when she plasters herself with the stuff worth three hundred ... you could be lucky. You can help yourself.'

Harry shook his head.

'No thanks ... I've got all I want. At my age, Jack, I've got beyond bothering about money. I'll do the job with pleasure but I don't want anything out of it.'

Bromhead stared at him.

'You've got all you want?' He leaned forward. 'Look, Harry, you could pick up at least a hundred grand out of this.'

He was thinking: *at my age I've got beyond bothering about money.* What the hell was happening to this goddamn world? How could anyone have too much?

Again Harry shook his head.

'I don't want it, Jack. I've got all I want. I like a simple life ... forget it. How do you want it done?'

Bromhead now became suspicious. He couldn't imagine any-one doing anything as big as this for nothing unless he had a nut loose.

'There has to be a motive, Harry,' he said, trying to make his voice sound patient. 'If there's no motive, the cops will start digging and that's something I don't want ... they could dig me up.'

Being a professional, Harry understood what Bromhead was saying.

'Okay ... so we have a motive ... keep talking ...'

'When you hit the old lady, you take her rings, her bracelets and her pearls. Keep them ... it's your pay-off, Harry.'

Harry moved restlessly.

'Not for me. I've got beyond that caper. What would I do with them? I've kissed the creeps who handle stuff like that goodbye. I won't want to be bothered. I have all the money I want. I'm doing this for you, Jack. I owe you and I pay my debts.'

This was something Bromhead couldn't believe.

'But, Harry ... for God's sake! You can't refuse more than a hundred big ones! You can't!'

As Bromhead said this, he was watching Harry and he saw Harry was suddenly looking bored and this frightened him.

'Suppose we skip this?' Harry said, his voice cold. 'Tell me how you want the job done and I'll do it.'

Bromhead began to sweat. He now had to accept the fact that this man, sitting before him, couldn't care less about money. To him, it was like looking at a man from the moon.

'Harry ... there has to be a motive,' Bromhead said, trying to control the unsteadiness of his voice. 'You must take her god-damn jewels.'

Harry shrugged.

'So, okay, I take her jewels. You can use them, can't you? I hit her ... that's okay. I told you I'd fix anything or anyone for you for what you did for me ... fine. So I take the jewels and I give them to you ... but they're not for me.'

Listening to the hard, impatient voice, Bromhead realized Harry meant what he was saying and to press him further could cause trouble.

He thought of Gerald. He had imagined it was only the young who didn't care about money ... now, for God's sake ... Harry was saying the same thing!

He gave up.

'Okay, Harry. Don't ever say I didn't make the offer. If that's the way you want it . . . that's the way you want it.'

'Let's cut the crap,' Harry said. 'Tell me how you want it done.'

Bromhead leaned forward, his hands on his knees.

'You have to get into the penthouse. It's tricky. The hotel dick buzzes around. No one get up there without the hall porter giving his say-so. You're good at impersonations . . . so, imagine you are a piano tuner . . .'

While this conversation was going on, Patterson was conducting Mrs Van Davis from his office and to the revolving doors to where her sleek Cadillac was waiting. Her chauffeur had the door open.

Mrs Van Davis had invested fifty thousand dollars on Patterson's advice in I.B.M. She was happy and Patterson pleased. He was able to endure her yakking, smile warmly down at her fat, wrinkled face, knowing he had done a good morning's work.

Once settled in the car, rather like a performing elephant settles on a stool, Mrs Van Davis waved her fat fingers, glittering with diamonds and he waved back. When the Cadillac had moved into the traffic, he heaved a sigh of relief and walked back to his office. That was his last appointment before lunch. He looked at his gold Omega, yet another present from Mrs Morely-Johnson, saw he had twenty-five minutes to clear his desk before lunching with Bernie Cohen.

It was now just under three weeks since he had handed Irving Fellows' secretary the forged will. During the first week, Patterson had been guilt ridden, but by now, he had come to accept the fact that nothing could happen until the old lady died and this could be some time ahead.

He told himself he must put this affair out of his mind. He had been impressed by Bromhead. This had been a surprise, of course – Bromhead and Sheila working together, but thinking about it, he saw how easily he had walked into the trap. He had only himself to blame. If he hadn't fallen for Sheila, this would never have happened. Patterson had a lot of resilience. It took him several days to recover from the shock, but now he had recovered. He had confidence in Bromhead. He admired the clever way Bromhead had suggested how he should take care of Abe Weidman who was, of course, the danger man. Bromhead had been right too when he had said the dead don't care. By the time the will was proved, Mrs Morely-Johnson would be cremated and the Cancer Research Fund, not knowing what they had missed, wouldn't grieve. The main thing was his own inheritance would remain undisturbed. It was now a matter of patient waiting and at his age, Patterson felt he could afford to wait.

He settled down behind his desk to sign papers, and as he signed he thought what he would have for lunch. As Bernie Cohen was picking up the tab, Patterson felt he might indulge himself. Perhaps a prawn cocktail with a touch of curry mayonnaise and a rognons flambés. A little heavy, Patterson thought, but this was what he fancied.

Vera Cross looked in.

'Mrs Morely-Johnson on the phone, Chris.'

Patterson grimaced.

'Okay ... put her on.'

What did she want? he wondered as he listened to the clicking on the line, then Mrs Morely-Johnson's raucous voice hit his eardrum and he hurriedly held the receiver away.

'Chris?'

'Good morning, Mrs Morely-Johnson. How are you?'

'I'm pretty well. I'm not getting any younger but I'm not complaining. I don't like people who are always complaining so I don't complain.'

'I agree with you.'

'And how are you?'

Patterson began to dig holes in his blotter with his paper knife.

'I'm fine, thank you. Was there something, Mrs Morely-Johnson?'

'When you talk like that, Chris, I know you are busy. Have I interrupted something?'

'Certainly not.' Patterson put down the paper knife. He realized he had allowed an impatient note to come into his voice and the old lady had spotted it ... that was bad tactics. 'You know I like nothing better than to do something for you.'

Mrs Morely-Johnson gave her shrill, girlish laugh that set Patterson's teeth on edge.

'Dear Chris! How nice of you! But I know how busy you are so I won't keep you. Could you come here at five o'clock? I want to consult you.'

Patterson glanced at his engagement book. He had an appointment with Jack Deakin at 16.00. Deakin, the director of the Splendid Hotel, wanted a loan. Patterson was sure he could get rid of him in half an hour, then he was free.

'It will be my pleasure,' he said.

'And Chris ...' There was a long pause while Patterson, now reading a letter he had to sign, waited.

'Yes, Mrs Morely-Johnson?'

'Please bring my will when you come.'

Patterson stiffened. The letter he was holding fluttered from his fingers to the floor. He couldn't believe he was hearing aright.

'I'm sorry.' He was aware his voice had turned husky. 'I didn't get that. The line seems bad. What did you say?'

'I can hear you clearly ... how odd. Please bring my will with you. I want to make changes.'

Patterson turned cold and his heart began to race.

'I am calling Mr Weidman,' Mrs Morely-Johnson went on. 'I want him to make a new will for me. I'm sure he will come at five this evening and then you and he can settle everything.'

Blind panic hit Patterson. For a long moment, he sat motionless, his hand like a claw, gripping the telephone receiver.

'Chris?' The squawking voice aroused him. 'Are you there?' He willed himself to think.

'Yes ... the line is very bad. I can't think why.' His brain was racing. He was like a fighter who has walked into a crushing punch and now weaved, dodged and ducked to survive. 'I'm afraid it can't be done as quickly as that, Mrs Morely-Johnson. Don't call Mr Weidman. I'm sorry, but to bring you your will ... there are formalities. When I come this evening I will bring you an authorization to sign. Our legal department won't release your will without your signature.'

'Oh, nonsense!' Mrs Morely-Johnson's voice rose a note. 'Mr Fellows is always very kind to me. Put me through to him. Of course he will let you have my will!'

Patterson shut his eyes. He knew Fellows wouldn't hesitate to hand the will over if Mrs Morely-Johnson asked him. Every Christmas the old lady sent his brats expensive presents and Fellows appreciated this.

'Mr Fellows isn't in today,' Patterson said, the lie bringing sweat beads to his face. 'Is this all that urgent? You have given us the will for safe keeping ... we do need your signature to release it, Mrs Morely-Johnson ... please may I ask you to understand?'

There was a long pause, then she said, sounding disgruntled, 'Oh, very well. I don't want to upset your silly bank ... then I must wait.'

Patterson took out his hankerchief and wiped his face.

'That's very understanding of you. I will bring the authorization at five. You will have the will tomorrow morning.'

'How tiresome!' She made no attempt to conceal her annoyance. 'I wanted to read it this evening.'

'You will have it without fail tomorrow morning, Mrs Morely-Johnson.'

'Oh, very well,' and she hung up.

Patterson grimaced and leaned back in his chair. The thought of a shrimp cocktail with a touch of curry mayonnaise, followed by rognons flambés now made him feel sick.

At 17.00, Patterson rang the bell of the penthouse. He had come armed with a plastic box containing four rare orchids. He knew from the tone of the old lady's voice that she would need softening.

Sheila opened the door and stood aside to let him in.

'I must talk to Bromhead,' Patterson said, his voice low. 'It's an emergency.'

He saw her flinch.

'He will be here when you leave.'

Patterson moved past her and out on to the terrace.

Sheila heard Mrs Morley-Johnson say, 'I'm annoyed with you, dear Chris. Come here and be scolded.' She went into her office and called Bromhead. 'Come to my room right away,' she said and hung up.

Patterson had guessed right. The orchids worked like a charm. Mrs Morely-Johnson was so pleased she forgot to remain cross. After some chit-chat that Patterson had to endure, she said, 'Chris, dear ... I've been thinking about Sheila. She is such a kind person, so considerate ... you can't imagine. I want to reward her ... that's why I want my will. I'm going to leave her a little money.'

Patterson's mind worked swiftly. The danger here was very real.

'That's no problem,' he said. 'A simple codicil will take care of that. I can arrange it for you. You don't have to bother Mr Weidman with this. I can add the codicil and have your signature witnessed. Absolutely no problem.'

Mrs Morely-Johnson put on her thick-lensed glasses and peered at him.

'I think Mr Weidman must do it, Chris. He always looks

after my legal work.'

Patterson shifted in his chair.

'That's as you wish, of course, but Mr Weidman will charge a fee. I can arrange this for you at no expense.' It was a last, desperate throw.

Mrs Morely-Johnson considered this. Had she been a greedy woman this would have been a telling point, but she wasn't. Patterson, his heart hammering, felt a chill run through him as she shook her head.

'That's very considerate of you, Chris, but I don't want to upset Mr Weidman. I must consult him. Do you think fifteen thousand dollars would be the right amount to leave Sheila?'

'That would be very generous,' Patterson said in a low, strangled voice.

'Good! Then give me this silly paper and I will sign it and I will call Mr Weidman right away ... then it will all be in order.'

Patterson was desperate now. He must talk to Bromhead ... he must gain time. As Mrs Morely-Johnson scrawled her signature on the paper he gave her, he said, 'Didn't you know? Mr Weidman left for New York this morning. I ran into him as he was leaving. He won't be back until Monday.'

Mrs Morely-Johnson threw up her beautiful, old hands.

'You see? Nothing is ever easy. Well, then I must wait, but bring me my will tomorrow, Chris, please.' She beamed at him. 'After all, as you said, it really isn't urgent. It's not as if I'm going to die tomorrow.'

'That's right,' Patterson said huskily.

'Would you like a drink? I think a little champagne would be nice. I'll call Sheila.'

Patterson couldn't stand any more of this. He got to his feet.

'Please excuse me. This is my busy period. I really must run along.'

He kissed her old hand, listened to her thanks for the orchids again, then left her. As he walked into the living-room, she turned on her tape recorder and sat back to listen to herself playing a Beethoven sonata.

Sheila was waiting in the vestibule. She motioned Patterson to her bedroom. He went into the room and found Bromhead sitting in one of the lounging chairs.

Sheila remained in the vestibule where she could watch Mrs Morely-Johnson.

Patterson closed the door.

'She's asking for her will,' he said, trying to control the panic in his voice. 'My legal department could become suspicious. To ask for the will twice in three weeks ... it doesn't make sense. The man in charge could telephone her.'

Bromhead nodded. His calm expression did something to damp down Patterson's panic.

'Why is she asking for the will?' he asked.

'She's leaving Sheila fifteen thousand. She insists Weidman handles it. I tried to talk her out of it, but she insists.'

Bromhead absorbed this, then again he nodded.

His calmness began to exasperate Patterson.

'She was about to call Weidman, but I stalled her. I told her Weidman had gone to New York until Monday.'

'Has he?' Bromhead asked.

Patterson shook his head.

'No.'

'That's dangerous.'

Patterson slammed his fist into the palm of his hand.

'What the hell else could I say?' His voice shot up. 'I had to stop her calling him until I had talked to you.'

'That's right.' Bromhead thought for a moment. Tomorrow was the twenty-first. He saw now he had timed the operation to the split second. 'Don't do anything ... just wait.'

'Don't do anything?' Patterson stared incredulously at Bromhead. 'What are you saying? I've got to do something!'

Bromhead waved his hand, signalling Patterson to keep his voice down.

'You are going to inherit one hundred thousand dollars a year for life,' he said quietly. 'That is all you have to think about. Don't do anything.'

'But she wants her will by tomorrow morning!'

'Do nothing. She won't need it.'

Patterson stared into the ice grey eyes and he felt a chill run through him.

'She'll expect it ... She...' Then he stopped.

Bromhead got to his feet.

'If you want your inheritance, Mr Patterson, you won't ask questions, but you will do what I suggest ... nothing.' He moved to the door, paused and stared at Patterson, 'But, of course, if you don't want one hundred thousand dollars a year for life then you will give the old lady the forged will, let her call Mr Weidman and explain what has happened. In my turn, I will give her the tape. This is something you must decide for yourself.'

Patterson felt the blood drain out of his face. He had a sudden presentiment that something was going to happen and this something was something he didn't want to know about.

'All right,' he said, his voice unsteady, 'if you really mean I'm to do nothing, then I'll do nothing. But when she calls me, what am I to say?'

'What makes you think she will call you?' Bromhead asked, turned and left the room.

Patterson, cold and frightened, realized he was now involved in something far worse than forgery, but the fingers of gold beckoned to him: one hundred thousand dollars a year for life! He had to think of himself. He had to rely on Bromhead. He was in too deep a trap not to have to rely on Bromhead.

He went into the vestibule and opened the front door. He saw Sheila on the terrace arranging the orchids in a vase. He crossed to the elevator and pressed the down button.

As he descended in the elevator, his mind was in a whirl. In a situation like this you can't just do nothing, he told himself and yet Bromhead had told him to do exactly that. Tomorrow morning, if he didn't do something, he knew Mrs Morely-Johnson would be telephoning asking him why he hadn't come.

If you want to keep your inheritance, Mr Patterson ... do nothing.

Since he had read Mrs Morely-Johnson's will he had thought about nothing else during his leisure moments than how he would use this massive inheritance. He would of course resign from the bank. He would scrap all his clothes and buy himself a complete new wardrobe. He would book a passage on the *Queen Elizabeth* for Europe. First, he would savour London. He would play around there, staying at the Dorchester Hotel, then he would move on to Paris, staying at the Plaza Athene. He was sure he wouldn't be lonely: with his looks and his money he would only have to lift an eyebrow and girls would materialize. Then two weeks at the Eden in Rome. By then he would have had enough of the city lights. He would head for Capri and relax in the sun. He would stay there during the season. Patterson loved the sun and from what he had heard, the Italian girls really know how to give out. From then on there would be time to make further plans, but this was the master plan to be put into operation immediately the inheritance was his.

But as the elevator took him to the ground floor, he was sick with anxiety. Do nothing? It seemed to him that his dreams and plans were falling to bitter pieces. He thought of Bromhead. The man seemed so confident. Do nothing? *Do nothing?*

The elevator doors swished silently open and he walked into the lobby.

'Hi, Chris!'

He came to an abrupt standstill, his heart skipping a beat. Advancing towards him, his fat face beaming was the last man he wanted to see: Abe Weidman. Somehow, he forced a smile, thrusting out his hand. As Weidman pumped it, he managed to say, 'This is a surprise, Abe. What are you doing here?'

'Just thought I'd drop by and see the old lady ... she likes attention.' Weidman winked. 'I wanted to take another look at those Picassos. Have you been to see her?'

'Yes.' For a long moment Patterson's mind refused to work. It bounced around inside his skull like a terrified mouse getting away from a cat. Then he got himself under control. 'Take my advice, Abe and skip it. She's in one of her bad moods.'

Weidman's eyebrows shot up.

'What's biting her?'

'God knows ... I don't have to tell you ... every so often she gets like this. Old age, I guess.' He caught hold of Weidman's arm. 'Come and have a drink with me.'

Weidman hesitated, then shrugged. 'Sure ... if she's like that.' He allowed himself to be steered towards the bar. As they were walking together across the lush carpet, Bromhead came out of the elevator. He saw them go into the bar and his eyes narrowed. This was getting dangerous. He turned and re-entered the elevator back to the penthouse.

As the elevator took him upwards, he told himself that he must now make arrangements for an unbreakable alibi.

He found Mrs Morely-Johnson settling herself before the piano. She was taking off her beautiful rings, making a little pile of them on the side of the Steinway. She looked up as Bromhead approached.

'Excuse me, madam.'

She peered at him.

'Is that you, Bromhead?'

'Yes, madam.'

She completed piling her rings and then struck C sharp. She smiled. Yes, she told herself, her touch remained constant. She struck E flat.

'What is it, Bromhead?'

'The Rolls needs servicing, madam. If you are agreeable, I

would like to take it to Los Angeles early tomorrow morning. I will have it back by five o'clock.'

'Los Angeles? Isn't that a long way to go?'

'It's the only garage I trust,' Bromhead said. 'A Rolls is a very special car, madam.'

'And you will be away all day? I can't remember ... have I any appointments, Bromhead?'

'I asked Miss Oldhill ... there are no appointments.'

She played a quick scale.

'Very well. Be sure you give yourself a good lunch, Bromhead.'

'Yes ... thank you, madam.'

Bromhead regarded her as she began to play. Although he had no ear for music, instinct told him he was listening to a performer of great talent.

He looked long and closely, because he liked the old lady and at this moment he sincerely wished she hadn't so much money for he knew he was looking at her for the last time ... this saddened him.

Seven

At one time, Joey Spick was considered the most efficient of Solly Marks's debt collectors. He was a bulky man with tremendous shoulders and short, thick legs. He looked as amiable as an enraged orang-outang. But now, through a misjudgement of human nature, he had become what Marks called 'deadwood'. He had been demoted to odd-job man with a social status no higher than the man with the dustpan and brush who runs behind circus horses ready to take care of trouble.

At one time Joey could terrorize any debtor. He had a neat trick which really scared the crap out of people behind in their payments. He would stand before them making a growling noise, then expand his muscles and the seams of his jacket would split. He kept a scared little tailor busy sewing the seams together again after he had given his demonstration. It was a terrifying performance and more often than not it produced immediate payment. If, however, the debtor just didn't have the money, then Joey would produce his length of piping.

Some five months ago, Joey had what seemed an easy assignment. He was told to collect two thousand dollars from a Chinese cook who was late in his payments. Joey was only cautious when he had to talk to men larger than himself, which was seldom, and this Chinese cook was old, brittle and apparently harmless. Joey looked forward to parting what was left of the old man's hair with his stick of lead.

He arrived at the restaurant, made his request while he lovingly fingered his cosh. The Chinaman bowed and said the money was ready and Joey felt frustrated. He followed the old man into the kitchen. Joey was pretty dull-witted. The saucepan on the stove half-full of boiling cooking fat meant nothing to him. The old man waved to the table where an envelope was lying. As Joey, off his guard, picked up the envelope, he received the hot fat in his unattractive face.

It took Joey some eight weeks in hospital to recover from this assault and by that time the Chinese cook had vanished into the blue, leaving Solly Marks minus two thousand dollars and minus his most reliable collector. It became obvious when Joey came out of hospital he wasn't going to be the same man as when he went in. Not only was he disfigured – that in itself wouldn't have been a bad thing because he now looked even more terrifying with white scars running down his puffy red face where the fat had caught him – but he had lost his morale. Although Marks started him off again as a debt collector, Marks quickly realized that Joey had lost his bite. Joey was now always looking for another saucepan of hot fat and he ran at any sign of opposition. Regretfully, Marks took him off debt collecting and made him an odd-job man and a man who merely did odd jobs for Marks was very poorly paid.

Marks believed in economizing when he could. He now had another I.O.U. for ten thousand dollars from Bromhead and he saw no reason why he shouldn't give Joey the chore of acting as second guard. He would only have to pay Joey forty bucks a week and the rest of the money would be profit and if there was anything Solly liked it was quick, large profits.

So Joey got the job of looking after Gerald during the night while Hank looked after him during the day. This was a chore that Joey found boring and hateful. For one thing he liked sitting in his favourite bar during the evening, tossing back cheap whisky; then he liked to go to bed: he was a great man for sleeping. To sit on an upright chair all the goddamn night outside Gerald's door was the worst job Marks had so far given him.

For the past twenty-nine days, Gerald had been held prisoner in what is called a walk-up, cold-water apartment. It was on the top floor of one of Marks's tenement buildings, strictly reserved for poor Blacks. The apartment consisted of a reasonably large room with a beat-up bed, a beat-up armchair, a table, an upright chair and a rented TV set. Off this room was a kitchen no bigger than a closet equipped with a greasy electric grill and a dirty, cracked sink. On the other side of the room was a shower and an ancient toilet: the flush worked from time to time, but not often: the shower dribbled cold water. There was a threadbare carpet on the floor of the main room which produced puffs of dust when walked on. The only window was boarded up by two bits of wood that allowed the minimum of hot summer air to infiltrate. The room was always unbearably hot and the noise coming from the other apartments practically drowned the sound of the television set even with the sound right up.

Gerald was used to living rough, but not this rough. Had he been better housed, provided with a girl, he might have been prepared to accept his kidnapping, but because Marks was too mean and wished to make a profit and had imprisoned him in this stinking slum, Gerald, his suppressed rage vicious, was determined to break out.

His first attempt had nearly succeeded, but he had been too confident. While Hank had been dozing in a room along the corridor, Gerald had managed to get the lock off the door with a knife he had found in the kitchen. Hank had checked the room twenty minutes later, found Gerald gone, raced down the stairs, got into his car and had had headed fast for the bus station. That had been Gerald's mistake. Thinking about it later, he realized the bus station would be the first place Hank would come looking for him. He wouldn't make that mistake again.

As he was boarding the bus, having spent his last few dollars on a ticket – dollars kept hidden in one of his shoes – Hank, beaming broadly had tapped him on his shoulder.

So great was Gerald's fear of this huge Negro that he went with him without fuss to the car and back to his prison. There, he received four violent slaps across his face – the fourth one knocking him cold.

Gerald came to to find that Hank had screwed a bolt on the outside of the door and further escape plans seemed frustrated until Joey Spick arrived.

Looking at Joey, knowing he was the night guard, Gerald's hopes of escape returned. He could see Joey was not only dull witted, but also a lush. It took only three nights for Gerald to find out that Joey fell asleep soon after 22.00, lulled by the rot-gut whisky he had brought with him to pass the night hours. He could hear Joey snoring. He knew Hank either was out or sleeping in a room at the end of the corridor and he began to formulate a plan.

Then one night he heard Hank talking to Joey in the corridor. Listening, his ear against the door, he learned on the night of the twentieth, Hank was visiting his girl-friend.

He heard Hank say, 'Watch this little bastard, Joey. I won't be back until after two. You hear me? You keep awake!'

'Waja mean?' Joey sounded indignant. 'When I do a job for Solly, I do it!'

'Okay ... so you keep awake!'

Gerald decided the next night then was the now or never attempt to break out.

The following evening, around 20.00, Joey unbolted the door, came into the room and slapped down a paper sack containing two greasy hamburgers which had been Gerald's staple diet for the past twenty-nine nights.

Gerald ignored him. He was watching television. There was a good western on, but Gerald scarcely noticed the action. He was very tense. Then Hank came to the open door. Hank was wearing a white suit, a black shirt with a pink tie with orange circles and an orange coloured straw hat. He stank of toilet water and after-shave and his black eyes glittered expectantly. He was going on the town with his girl who he knew would give out at the end of the evening.

'Sleep tight, baby,' he said to Gerald. 'Dream of me. I'll give you a blow-by-blow account tomorrow.'

Gerald didn't look around. Shrugging, Hank left and Joey leaned against the wall to see the last moments of the film. The final gun battle didn't impress him.

'Punks,' he muttered under his breath. 'Actor punks,' and he went out, shutting the door and shooting the bolt.

Leaving the television on, Gerald ate the hamburgers. He now had no money and he didn't know when he would get his next meal. Somehow he had to reach Sheila. She was the only one who would help him. He was smoulding with rage and vicious-ness. He was now determined to blow Bromhead's smart money-making plan sky-high. Nothing now would please him more than to fix Bromhead for what he had done to him. He would see his goddamn aunt and tell the stupid old cow about Brom-head and Patterson, but he wouldn't mention Sheila. He would see Sheila first, warn her what he was going to do so she could get out. When he had convinced his aunt, he would join Sheila and they would go back to New York together. Sheila would get her job back at the hospital and they would forget all this crap about having a million dollars. Who the hell wanted a million dollars? With the money Sheila made as a nurse, they could live all right together. He might even try to make some money him-self – just how, he didn't know, but he would think about it later.

The thing was to escape from this stinking room, get to the Plaza Beach Hotel, tell Sheila, then talk to his aunt.

Soon after 23.30, he heard Joey's strangled snoring. Sweating and tense, Gerald looked at his watch. In another hour he would start his escape plan. He wanted Joey to be in a deep, whisky sleep. He waited, lying on his bed and as he waited, he thought of Sheila. He was sure she didn't know the way he was being treated. He was sure she wouldn't stand for him being kept in a goddamn slum like this. She was tricky ... he had to admit that. He had had nearly a month on his own to do noth-ing but watch television and think. He had come up with a lot of ideas and these ideas he would have to persuade Sheila to accept. He had to convince her that the people running this stinking world had to go. This system of living entirely for money, thinking only of money, living a blind rat-in-a-cage life for money had to go. The scene had to be changed. All these lying politicians, the rich, the people who had power to say this and that and make it stick had to go. The old, useless people who lived on dividends, they had to go too: the non-produc-tive. He wanted to make a clean sweep of them all! Anyone over sixty years of age was so much waste of food. He wanted them all shoved into gas ovens. Imagine! No more old men, no more old women cluttering up the streets: just the young ... what a marvellous world that could be! How marvellous to go into the streets and find no old people! The scene had to be changed. He was eager to talk to Sheila and to convince her.

But, first he had to get out of here.

At 23.40, he went silently into the kitchen, took a knife from a drawer and returned to his room. He stripped the bed until he reached the bare, lumpy mattress. He dug holes in the mattress, pulling out the kapok in small tufts. Then, satisfied, he moved to the door and listened. He could hear Joey snoring. Again he went silently into the kitchen, opened a cupboard and lifted out an iron frying-pan: it made a solid weapon. He balanced it in his hand, then returning to the room, he looked at his watch. He wouldn't wait any longer. With his heart beating unevenly, he put the frying-pan on the floor by the door, took a box of matches from his pocket, struck a match and ignited one of the tufts of kapok. He ignited four other tufts, then stood back.

He had reasoned, when thinking up this plan of escape, that by setting fire to the kapok he would create a great deal of smoke. He would then yell for Joey who would come blundering into the smoke and Gerald, waiting against the wall would hit him on the head with the frying-pan, then bolt down the stairs and away. It seemed to him that this was pretty fool-proof, but it didn't work that way. The kapok was years old and as dry as tinder. It certainly produced a lot of smoke, but also a terrifying sheet of flame. The flame leapt up, and in a moment or so, the wall by the bed was blazing.

Feeling the scorching heat, Gerald, choking from the smoke and in a panic, battered on the door, screaming to be let out.

Joey came awake. He had drunk a half bottle of whisky and he had been dreaming. When he drank too much he always dreamed of the Chinese cook. In his dream he again felt the hellish agony as the hot fat hit his face. He came awake with such a start that he fell off his chair and sprawled on the floor. He saw smoke billowing out from under the door. He heard the crackling of flames as they took hold of the dry, rotten walls. He felt the heat and terror gripped him. He heard Gerald screaming to be let out. Too drunk to think, feeling the heat, choking in the smoke, hearing people yelling to one another, realizing he was on the top floor and it was a long run down, Joey stumbled to his feet and not caring a damn for anyone or anything except his own safety, he went blindly down the five flights of stairs, kicking, hitting and cursing anyone who got in his way.

By the time he reached the street, the top floor of the tenement building was a furnace of flames.

Around 20.00 on the same evening Bromhead was giving Harry Miller his final instructions. They were together in the motel cabin. The shades were drawn and both men were drinking Vat 69.

Harry had shown Bromhead the piano tuner's equipment he had bought which consisted of several tuning forks, a number of piano tuning keys, a selection of piano wire and so on.

'This is jumping the gun a little, Harry,' Bromhead said. 'Her regular piano tuner isn't due until next month, but Sheila will fix that. She can talk the old girl into anything. You have to be careful of the hall porter, he has a good memory. It wouldn't surprise me if he knows when the piano tuner is due to come, so watch that. You have the card I gave you!'

'Don't make so much of this,' Harry said a little irritably. 'I can handle any goddamn hall porter.'

'I'm just warning you. I don't want a last minute slip up.'

'When I say I'll do something, you can consider it done.'

Bromhead nodded.

'Okay, Harry. All the same, I'd like to go over the routine again. You arrive at ten o'clock. You go to the desk, tell the hall porter who you are, show your card and cope with him if he turns tricky. He will call the penthouse. Sheila will answer. She'll say it's okay for you to come up. You go up. The old lady will be around, either on the terrace or in the living-room where the piano is. Sheila will let you in. You knock her out.' Bromhead paused and regarded Harry. 'You can do this without hurting her? She won't know it is going to happen, but I don't want her hurt.'

'That's no problem,' Harry said. 'A small bruise that'll look good . . . she won't know what hit her.'

'You strap her with tape and leave her in the vestibule. You then take care of the old lady. You take her jewellery. You wait in the penthouse for at least twenty minutes – you're supposed to be fixing the piano – then you leave. You come back here, get rid of your disguise, put the jewels in the box I've given you and mail it to Solly Marks. You've got his address?'

Harry nodded.

'Unless, of course, Harry, you change your mind and want to keep the stuff. I'd like you to keep it.'

'I don't want it.'

Bromhead shrugged.

'Okay, so you don't want it. You have your return ticket?'

'Don't fuss, Jack. I have the scene. It will be done. You didn't fuss when you pulled me out of that gang-up.' Harry stared at him. 'This makes us quits.'

'Okay, Harry, but it worries me you get nothing out of this.'

'I'm fine as I am.'

There was a long pause, then Bromhead said, 'There is a little problem. I'd like to fill you in about Sheila. Like me, she's money hungry. When I told her the possibilities she didn't hesitate, but now, I get the feeling she is hesitating. The trouble is, Harry, the old girl has a way with her. If she was an old bitch like most of the rich old women in this town, it wouldn't be so tough. You following me?'

Harry sipped his drink.

'Keep talking.' The cold flat note in his voice told Bromhead that Harry had no scruples. That was okay with Bromhead. This was a job for a man with no scruples.

'Sheila doesn't know what is going to happen, but she's no fool. I have an idea she suspects what is going to happen. You must watch this. She could lose her nerve.'

'What does that mean?' Harry asked.

'Possibly a complication. I've been thinking about it. No matter how carefully an operation is planned, something can turn up to hitch it. My thinking is this: suppose at the last moment, Sheila loses her nerve. What does she do? She gets a call from the hall porter telling her you have arrived. If her nerve holds, she will tell him to send you up. If her nerve doesn't hold, she will say it isn't convenient for you to come up and that will be that. There is no way for you to get up to the penthouse unless she says so. Don't try it. She may say it's okay for you to come up, then lose her nerve and not answer the door when you ring. Ring once: don't keep ringing as that could alert the old lady. Just ring once and if Sheila doesn't answer the door, walk down to the next floor. There's a fire staircase on this floor. You go up the stairs and you can get into Sheila's room. The door is bolted, but I have loosened the screws. All you have to do is to lean on the door and it will open. Take care of Sheila first, then go ahead with the job.'

Harry finished his drink. He sat for a long moment, thinking.

'It's a damn funny thing,' he said, 'you get an assignment that looks easy and suddenly it isn't. Well, okay. So if this broad loses her nerve and doesn't give the hall porter the green light, I do nothing . . . is that it?'

'There's nothing else to do. You won't get up to the penthouse without her say-so, but I'm looking for trouble, Harry. I'm pretty sure this won't happen. I'm going back now and I'm talking to her. I've got a screw to turn and now's the time to turn it. I just want you to be fully in the photo.'

'So if this flops ... I go back home?'

'Stick around for a week, Harry ... I could think up another idea. I'm not worried about this. It'll work, but I believe in looking ahead and thinking of possible trouble.'

'Okay. I like it here ... makes a change from New York. I'll stick around.'

Bromhead got to his feet.

'Ten o'clock tomorrow then.'

'That's it.'

The two men shook hands and Bromhead left. He drove back to the Plaza Beach Hotel, reached his room, then put through a call to the penthouse.

When Sheila answered, he said, 'I want to talk. Can you come down to my room?'

'I can't get away,' Sheila said, 'but it's all right for you to come up. She has friends.'

Bromhead let himself into the penthouse. He could hear voices on the terrace and caught a quick glimpse of four people playing cards. He went straight to Sheila's bedroom.

'What is it?' Sheila asked as he came in. She was standing by the window and he could see she was nervous and strained.

'We have to talk,' Bromhead said. 'Your boy-friend has got us into trouble.'

She stiffened.

'Gerald? What's happened?'

Bromhead sat on the bed and waved her to the lounging chair.

'Sit down.'

She hesitated, then obeyed.

'I told you this was a long-term operation,' Bromhead said. 'The way I figured it, it looked good and simple. Up to now, it has worked: you fixed Patterson: I fixed the will. All we had to do, the way I saw it, was to sit it out and wait for the old lady to die ... that was the plan, but it is not working out like this because of Gerald. He had landed us both in serious trouble. I admit it is partly my fault. By the way he was behaving, I had to put him on ice. I had to get him out of the way where he couldn't become a nuisance. I made a mistake. I went to a man who agreed to take care of Gerald. This man was well recommended. I thought he was safe, but he has found out that you and I work for the old lady and he knows how wealthy she is. He is putting on the bite. He has Gerald locked up somewhere. Now he is asking for thirty thousand dollars.'

Sheila leaned forward.

'You mean he has Gerald a prisoner?'

'That's what I'm telling you. This man is dangerous. No thirty thousand dollars ... no Gerald. This man won't hesitate to knock Gerald on the head and dump him in the sea. I'm not being an alarmist. I'm stating facts.' As she began to speak, Bromhead held up his hand, stopping her. 'I've done a deal with him. I had to ... there was no other alternative. Now listen carefully ... tomorrow morning at ten o'clock a man will arrive to repair the Steinway. The hall porter will ask you if he can come up and you will say it's okay.' Bromhead paused and stared bleakly at Sheila. 'When he rings the bell, you will let him in. That's all you have to do. It's not difficult, but I want to know now that you will do it.'

Her face white, her eyes wide, Sheila asked, 'Where is Gerald?'

Bromhead made an impatient movement.

'Never mind about him. He's all right now, but if you don't do what I'm telling you ... if you don't let this man in ... then Gerald won't be all right.'

'Suppose I let this man in ... what will he do?'

'He will take some of the old lady's jewels. At ten o'clock, she is always on the terrace. She won't even know he has come and gone. He will gag and bind you. You don't have to worry ... he won't hurt you. He will go to her bedroom, take her jewel box and leave. It's as simple as that. When the police arrive, they will question you. You will say you thought the old lady had called the piano people. It never occurred to you to check with her. The jewels will be sold and you and I will be out of hock and Gerald will be free. Then, later, you two can go off together and wait until the old lady dies.'

She regarded him for a long moment.

'Suppose she sees this man?'

'That's not likely. You know as well as I do, she is always on the terrace at that time.'

Sheila shuddered.

'No! I'm not going to do it! I wish I had never met you! No!'

'I think you will have to,' Bromhead said, a sudden edge to his voice. 'If you don't care about Gerald, you might care what could happen to you. You're in this thing too deep now to back out. If I tell this man you won't play, he'll fix you. A squirt of acid can do a lot of damage. It comes without warning. You're

walking along a street, in a Self-service store, getting into a taxi
... then your face is finished, and if you're unlucky, your eyes
too.'

She shook her head.

'No!'

'Use your brains,' he went on. 'The old lady is so rich if she
loses some of her jewels, she can always replace them and they
are insured anyway.' He got to his feet. 'You now know the
situation. Just remember at ten o'clock, you hold Gerald's life in
your hands. It sounds dramatic, doesn't it? Like a bad TV
movie, but it happens to be a fact. I have to pay this money. If
you don't mind acid in your face, you should think of him.'

He went from the room and closed the door behind him.

Hank Washington ran his great hand down the Mulatto's
slim back as his mind dwelt on what was going to happen in
another hour. As the three-piece band began turning on the
heat, the sudden clanging of fire-bells and police sirens made
him miss a step.

'Steady, ole baby,' the Mulatto whispered, pressing her body
against his. 'Watch it, baby.'

Hank shifted his hand lower and squeezed her firm buttocks,
but his ears were pricked as more police sirens sounded.

'What's cooking?' he muttered as he saw the other Negro
dancers coming to a stop as they stared out of the big windows
into the street.

'Should you care, ole baby?' the Mulatto asked, her fingers
caressing his thick neck.

Hank looked across at the bar and saw the barman waving to
him. Gripping the girl around her slim waist, he shoved his way
across the dance floor to the bar.

The barman knew Hank was one of Solly Marks's men. Hank
was a special customer in the bar and a heavy tipper, but not for
nothing. The barman, an ex-boxer with scar tissue over his eyes,
who had once gone six rounds with Joe Louis, kept Hank in-
formed of anything within a mile radius of the bar that might
be useful to Marks's organization.

'Deacon's building is going up like a torch,' the barman told
Hank.

Hank reacted to this information like a man goosed with a
hot iron. His hand slid away from the girl's body, his eyes grew
round, then shoving the girl from him, he ran out of the bar
and on to the street.

At the far end of the waterfront he could see the flames and the smoke. Already the traffic had been stopped. Police were everywhere. He saw he couldn't use his car. Cutting down a side alley, he ran with long, looping strides, making fast ground, until he came within a hundred yards of the burning tenement block. He stopped short as the scorching heat hit him. It was impossible to go further forward. The narrow street was covered with coils of hose-pipe. The barman's description was no exaggeration. Flames and smoke poured from every window of the five storey building.

Hank stood, staring. Maybe Joey had got the little bastard out, he was thinking. He had better get to a telephone and alert Marks. Then Joey Spick emerged out of the smoke. Hank realized that Joey was pretty drunk and also scared. He grabbed hold of him.

'What's cooking?'

Joey choked and coughed. His eyes were red rimmed from smoke and he stared stupidly at Hank, for the moment not recognizing him, then when Hank shook him, he gulped and his eyes became less wild.

'He's gone!' he said. 'He set the room on fire! I couldn't do nothing! The goddamn place went up like a goddamn bonfire!'

'He's gone?' Hank snarled. 'You mean you let him get away?'

'No! He's dead! I tried to get the door open. He was in there yelling ... he's dead!'

Hank slapped Joey's scarred face, sending him reeling.

'You were sleeping, you sonofabitch!'

Joey cringed away.

'I guess I dozed off for a few moments. I tried to get him out ... the door was red-hot.' Joey snivelled. 'It wasn't my fault, Hank. I swear it wasn't my fault. The punk set the room on fire!'

Hank glared murderously at him.

'Too bad for you, Joey,' he said softly. 'Solly won't need you any more. Get your skates on and start rolling out of town.'

Leaving Joey, he walked around the side streets until he found one of the Negro tenants he knew. The Negro confirmed that there were ten dead: all from the top and fourth floors. Hank grimaced. Solly wouldn't be pleased. He made his way back to the night club where he could use the telephone.

The Mulatto girl was dancing with a young, thin Negro who, seeing Hank come into the club, released the girl as if she were red-hot and vanished through the emergency exit. Everyone who frequented the club knew that it was bad medicine even to look at Hank's girl.

Hank glared at the girl who smiled at him, then he shut himself in a telephone booth. He called Marks's house. He was told Mr Marks was on his way back from 'Frisco and his plane wouldn't arrive until 01.00. Hank said it was urgent and for Marks to call him as soon as he got in. He left the number of the night club. Then he joined the Mulatto.

They danced until 03.00, then Hank decided he wasn't going to wait any longer. Marks hadn't called and Hank felt it was time he took the Mulatto to her bed.

It wasn't until 09.15 the following morning that Solly Marks learned that not only Bromhead's problem child had gone up in flames but also that he had lost a tenement building that was under-insured.

At 07.00 on the morning of the twenty-first of the month, the Plaza Beach Hotel came to action stations like a warship signalled: *Full ahead*. The quiet, efficient dynamo that was the heart of the hotel abruptly switched into top gear.

The four under-chefs in the vast kitchen began preparing for the breakfast rush: each had his special duty. Eggs, grilled ham, grilled bacon, waffles, bread for toast, gallons of orange juice, coffee and tea, cold ham, devilled kidneys were in preparation.

The night staff had already hosed down the drive and were changing with the day staff. Herman Lacey, the Director of the hotel, was in his office with the *maître d'hôtel* and the head chef planning the lunch and dinner menus. The night hall porter was gladly surrendering his office to the day hall porter, a large, fleshy-faced man known to the clients as George and who happened to own two hotels in Switzerland and a Bistro in Paris. George was a known character along the Pacific coast. He had an encyclopaedic mind. No matter what question was thrown at him, he immediately came up with an answer. *Time* magazine had once done an interview on him, calling him 'The Phenomenal George'.

The cleaners had gone. The hotel was spick and span. Already the first telephone calls for breakfast were coming through to the service room. As usual, Fred Lawson, the hotel detective, was the last of the staff to put in an appearance and he found Joe Handley waiting impatiently. Lawson grunted a good morning, then picked up the telephone receiver and ordered his usual waffles, grilled ham, four eggs and toast.

Handley reported that it had been a quiet night with only one drunk to cope with. Lawson grunted again.

'I guess I'll take a swim,' Handley said. 'It's going to be hot today.'

Lawson wasn't interested. He settled his bulk behind his desk and opened the morning newspaper. Handley left him.

Handley was a man who thrived on little sleep. Usually, he spent most of the morning on the beach, then after a light lunch, he went to bed and slept until 19.00 when he took over from Lawson. He went across to the staff quarters to change into swimming trunks.

At 08.00 Mrs Morely-Johnson was aroused by a gentle tap on her door. The bulky, smiling floor waitress, Maria, came in and set down the breakfast tray on the bedside table. Mrs Morely-Johnson beamed on her. She had spent a disturbed night and she was now glad to see the sunshine again: the kind of night old people often have: stupid dreams, the need to get up to go to the toilet, thoughts of the past and feeling sad about living alone. She was glad to see Maria; this large woman soothed her with her flashing smile and her genuine kindness. She was also glad to have her breakfast. As she poured her tea, she looked with pleasure at the crisp toast and the lightly boiled egg. That she might die in two hours time never entered her head.

In his apartment, Patterson also had slept badly. *Do nothing.* Bromhead had said. Well, he had done nothing, but his mind was in a torment. He couldn't forget Bromhead's cold, calm look as he had said: *What makes you think she will call you?* Patterson threw off the sheet and got out of bed. He began to pace around his bedroom. Of course she would call him, asking why he hadn't brought her her will ... unless ... Patterson flinched. Had he got himself involved in a murder plot? His mind shied away from such a thought, but the writing was on the wall. Unless she died, she would call him. There could be no other solution. He had to face the stark fact: Bromhead and Sheila planned to murder the old lady! They were both ruthless enough to do it! They stood to gain one million, five hundred thousand dollars!

He looked at the telephone. Call the police and tell them what he suspected? He thought of the tape. If he called the police and there was an investigation he would lose his inheritance and his job. He found he was so unnerved that he went into the living-room and poured himself a large brandy. The effect of the spirit stiffened his nerves. After all, he told himself, she is very old. She can't last more than a year or so and his life was before him. He was only guessing. There could be another solution. He must put this out of his mind. It was nothing to do with him. He must wait. He went into the kitchenette and plugged in the coffee percolator.

At 08.10, Bromhead was dressed, wearing his immaculate Hawes & Curtis uniform. He had had a good breakfast and was now ready to take the Rolls to Los Angeles. Leaving his room, he walked over to the garage. The Negro attendant nodded and smiled. Bromhead was liked by all the hotel staff.

'You're up early, Mr Bromhead,' he said. 'I've only just washed her.'

'She needs tuning,' Bromhead said, 'and a new set of plugs. She's not pulling as she should. I'm taking her to L.A. The Ace garage is the only one I know who can handle her.'

'That's correct, Mr Bromhead ... The Ace is sure good with top-class cars.'

Bromhead got into the Rolls, waved to the attendant and drove from the garage. As he drove along the coast road to Los Angeles, he first thought of Sheila. He felt sure that she would do as he had told her. Then he thought of his future: five hundred thousand dollars would bring comfort, security and new horizons. Not once did he think of Mrs Morely-Johnson.

Sheila, knowing she wouldn't sleep, had taken two sleeping pills and she woke, drowsy and languid. She had been dreaming of Gerald, of the time they had shared her small apartment in New York and with her eyes still closed, she reached out her hand to feel for him as she usd to do, then opened her eyes to look around the comfortable bedroom and her mind jerked back to the present. Then she remembered this was the day.

All you have to do is to let him in when he rings the bell.

So simple!

He will gag and bind you.

She flinched. Then she thought of Gerald. She thought of Bromhead's bleak eyes. *A squirt of acid in your face. Your face is finished ... if you're unlucky, your eyes too.* To be blind! She thought of the old lady groping her way around, peering at things. *She is so rich she can always replace her jewels ... anyway they are insured.*

But it was a betrayal. She had come to like the old lady. She had been the first person who had really been kind to her. She lay still, trying to make up her mind. *All you have to do is to let him in.* She realized it was impossible at this moment to make a decision. She got out of bed and went into the bathroom. As she stood under the shower, letting the tepid water cool her feverish body, she wondered how she was going to endure the next long two hours ahead of her.

Harry Miller slept peaceably until 08.00. After shaving and showering, he put on his make-up. While he gummed hairs to his upper lip, he hummed under his breath. Harry was completely relaxed. This was just another day's work for him. It needed finesse, of course, but he had finesse. It amused him that a man like Bromhead seemed so anxious. There must be a lot of money involved. Harry was glad that money no longer meant anything to him. He was glad to be out of the rat race. He was glad too that he would be able to get out of Bromhead's debt. He would return to New York and live out his life as he wanted to with nothing to bother his conscience. He regarded himself in the mirror ... perfect. He nodded his satisfaction. He put on a shabby, light weight grey suit, polished his black shoes, inspected the cuffs of his white shirt and decided he was part perfect. He then left the cabin, crossed to the restaurant, aware that it was going to be a hot, fine day. He took a corner table by the window and studied the menu. A killing job always give him an appetite. This interested him. He was aware that he was always ravenously hungry before doing a job. To the waitress's surprise, he ordered a steak with French fried potatoes, waffles with syrup and a pint of milk.

With plenty of time to spare, he lingered over the meal, then having paid his check, he packed his bag, took the piano tuner's outfit with him and got into the Hertz rented car.

He reached the Plaza Beach Hotel parking lot at 09.45. At this time in the morning there was plenty of space and he parked the car so he would have only a short distance to walk and could leave in a hurry if it was necessary.

The Negro parking attendant came over and eyed him suspiciously. It was his job to make sure only people to do with the hotel used the parking lot.

'You got business here, mister?' he demanded.

Harry nodded.

'You bet I have. I've got to fix a piano, but I'm ahead of time. Okay for me to wait here?'

'Sure, mister,' and his curiosity satisfied, the Negro returned to his wooden hut.

At three minutes to 10.00, Harry walked briskly up the steps and across the hotel lobby to the hall porter's desk. At this time in the morning, the lobby was bare of clients. Only three bell-hops were standing around, trying to look busy. George, the hall porter, was checking the Stock-market prices in the *Pacific Tribune*. He looked up as Harry came to the desk. His sharp, experienced eyes took in Harry's shabby suit and his little black bag and he decided this was no one of importance.

'Morning,' Harry said and laid the business card that Bromhead had given him on the desk. 'Mrs Morely-Johnson, please.'

George picked up the card and examined it. It told him that Mr Tom Terring, representative of Scholfield & Matthews, suppliers of pianos, organs and harps, stood before him.

George regarded Harry and what he saw he didn't like. He didn't like the heavily dyed black hair, nor the small restless eyes. He didn't like the shabby suit.

'This you?' he asked, tapping the card.

'That's me,' Harry said. 'Where do I find Mrs Morely-Johnson . . . what floor?'

'If you're trying to sell her a piano you're wasting your time.'

Harry laughed.

'Nothing like that. We had a call late yesterday. She has a broken piano wire. I'm here to fix it.'

George frowned. There was something about this man that worried him.

'You're not the usual guy who comes . . . a fellow named Chapman.'

'That's right. Chapman tunes pianos . . . I mend them.'

George shrugged. He picked up the telephone receiver and asked the operator to connect him with the penthouse.

Her toilet completed, Mrs Morely-Johnson wandered out on to the terrace. The time was 09.30. She had nothing to do now Bromhead had taken the Rolls to Los Angeles. She sat in the sun, looking across at the harbour and wondered how she could pass the next hours before going down to the grillroom where she had arranged lunch with friends.

She decided to clean her rings. Since she was half blind, this chore was always badly done, but she liked to do it. She often said to Sheila: 'I must never become a parasite. I have no patience with women who don't do *something* for themselves.'

'Sheila?' the raucous voice made Sheila stiffen. She came out on to the terrace.

'Yes, Mrs Morely-Johnson.'

'Will you be a dear and bring me my rings? I want to clean

them.'

Sheila felt her heart skip a beat. She looked furtively at her watch. Then she was suddenly glad. She knew the old lady loved her rings more than the rest of her jewellery. Her rings were kept in a special box. At least this man who was coming wouldn't now get them. The diamond brooches, the strings of pearls, the diamond necklaces would satisfy him.

She went into the old lady's bedroom, got the ring box and collected the cleaning material. She laid these out on the terrace table.

Mrs Morely-Johnson peered at everything to make sure she could find what she needed and nodded her satisfaction.

'Thank you, my dear.' She opened the ring box, then looked up and peered at Sheila. 'You are very quiet this morning. Are you feeling all right?'

'I have a slight headache,' Sheila said huskily and again looked at her watch. The time now was 09.56.

'Wretched things ... headaches. Go and lie down. Take an aspirin. When I was your age, I used to get a lot of headaches ... it's all part of a woman's burden.' She picked up a magnificent diamond and ruby ring and peered at it.

'I think I will,' Sheila said and returned to the living-room. Her hands were damp and her heart was thumping. She looked with dread at the telephone. She must think of Gerald, she told herself. What a fool she had been to have ever listened to Bromhead! She was sure he wasn't bluffing. How could a man bluff with a face like that? What did it matter if the old lady lost some of her jewels? And yet she felt ashamed. This was a betrayal of trust.

The telephone bell rang.

When Solly Marks learned that Gerald Hammett had died in the tenement fire, he realized this was information that must be relayed immediately to Bromhead. Marks was a man of swift action. He called Bromhead's room. Getting no answer, he called the hotel garage. The attendant told him that Bromhead was on his way to Los Angeles and had left around 08.20. Marks reckoned that Bromhead couldn't reach Los Angeles for another two hours. He telephoned Sergeant Pete Jackson, the traffic control officer at Los Angeles. Marks had good contacts with the police and the key men always received a turkey and two bottles of Scotch on Thanksgiving Day: these presents paid off in an emergency.

'Pete? This is Solly. Do me a favour?'

'Name it and it's yours.'

'There's a Rolls on the highway heading this way. No. P.C. M.J. 1. Dark red,' Marks said. 'I want the chauffeur ... Jack Bromhead ... to get to the nearest telephone fast and call me. Top priority, Pete.'

'Nothing to it,' Jackson said. 'One of my men will pick him up in five minutes.'

'Thanks, Pete,' and Marks hung up.

Bromhead had a nasty shock when a patrol officer on a powerful motor-cycle cut in ahead of him and flagged him down. Bromhead had been driving at a sedate forty-five miles an hour so he knew he wasn't being stopped for speeding. He glanced at the clock on the dashboard. It showed 09.45. Whatever the cop wanted, Bromhead decided it was a good thing he was being stopped. What better alibi than to be stopped by a cop some fifty miles or so from the scene of a murder?

The cop leaned into the car and stared at Bromhead.

'You Jack Bromhead?' he asked.

'Yes.'

'Got a message for you. You're to call Mr Solly Marks. It's urgent. There's a call-box about a mile head.'

Bromhead felt the muscles in his face turn stiff. A sudden cold, empty feeling developed in the pit of his stomach.

'Right ... thanks,' he said and engaged gear.

The cop went ahead, riding at sixty miles an hour and Bromhead kept up with him. The cop waited long enough to see Bromhead make his connection, then with a wave of his hand, he rode off.

'Solly? What's up?' Bromhead asked.

'There's been a fire. Your problem went up in the flames,' Marks said. 'He's deader than an amputated leg.'

Bromhead absorbed the shock. He knew Marks by now. If Marks said Gerald was dead ... he was dead.

'Okay, Solly,' he said and hung up.

In an emergency, Bromhead was always able to think swiftly and act promptly. With Gerald dead, his plan was in pieces. There would be no one million five hundred thousand dollars to be divided. The time was 09.58. In two minutes time Harry would be arriving at the hotel. In ten minutes time, probably less, the old lady would be dead. He must alert Sheila. Dropping a coin in the box, he dialled the number of the Plaza Beach Hotel. As he listened to the ringing tone, he glanced at his watch. It was now 10.00 The hotel operator said: 'The Plaza Beach Hotel. Good morning. Can I help you?'

'Connect me with Mrs Morely-Johnson,' Bromhead said.

'Yes, sir. Hold a moment.'

There was a long pause. Bromhead watched the cars as they roared along the highway and he was aware of a trickle of sweat running down his face.

'The line is busy, sir,' the operator told him. 'Will you hold on?'

Harry!

'I'll hold on,' Bromhead said.

He stood tense. Harry had arrived! The hall porter would check with Sheila. She would say it was okay for Harry to come up. It took less than a minute for Harry to get up to the penthouse by the express elevator. He would ring the bell and Sheila would let him in.

Then Bromhead heard the dialling tone and realized that he had been cut off. The bitch of a girl had pulled the plug on him! He found another coin, dropped it into the box and with a shaking finger, dialled again.

'The Plaza Beach Hotel. Good morning. Can I help you?'

Bromhead longed to get his fingers around this stupid bitch's throat and strangle her.

'You cut me off. I want Mrs Morely-Johnson,' he said, his voice a croak.

'I'm sorry, sir. I'm putting you through now. Mrs Morely-Johnson?'

'Yes!'

'Hold a moment, please.'

Eight

Joe Handley had enjoyed his swim and sun bathe. Now he walked up the steps to the hotel to pick up a copy of the *Pacific Herald* to catch up with the day's news.

As he entered the lobby, he saw an undersized man wearing a

shabby suit and carrying a small black bag leaving the hall porter's desk. Two things immediately struck Handley's police-trained mind. One was the black, heavily dyed hair and the other was that although this man had a fat face, as he walked across the lobby to the elevator, turning his back on Handley, he revealed a thin, stringy neck. Also, Handley's built-in cop instinct told him this was a man he didn't like.

As the elevator door swished to, cutting the man from Handley's sight, he walked over to George's desk.

'Who was that?' he asked.

'Some guy from Scholfield & Matthews to repair Mrs Morely-Johnson's piano,' George told him.

'Where's Lawson?'

'Where do you expect?' George had a low opinion of Fred Lawson. 'Taking a nap or stuffing his gut again.'

'I didn't like the look of that guy ... did you?'

George scratched his jaw.

'He can't help his looks, can he? I checked with Miss Oldhill. She said it was okay for him to go up.' George hesitated, then went on. 'But you're right, Joe ... there was something about him.'

The two men looked at each other. Handley hesitated. This wasn't his business. Lawson was in charge now.

'Miss Oldhill said it was okay?'

'That's right ... sounds as if she had a cold ... very husky.'

Again, Handley hesitated, then shrugging, he wandered over to the newspaper kiosk and bought the *Pacific Herald*. While he glanced at the headlines, he thought of the man who had just gone up to the penthouse. Why was it his instinct told him this man should be investigated? Something in the walk? The slightly hunched shoulders as if he expected someone to call after him?

It might be an idea to go up and check. The old lady was their most valued client. Lawson would blow a fuse, of course, if he found out. Check? How could he check? Carrying the newspaper, Handley went over to a chair and sat down. He couldn't bring himself to leave the lobby and go to his room. An instinctive alarm bell was ringing at the back of his mind.

It took him four minutes of hard thinking to solve the problem of his alarm. This man not only had a fat face and a thin neck, not only heavily dyed hair, but he was also wearing built-up shoes! Handley dropped the newspaper and got to his feet. He was going to check and to hell with Lawson!

Sheila listened to George's fruity baritone voice. She was shaking and could scarcely hold the telephone receiver.

'I understand, Miss Oldhill, that Mrs Morely-Johnson's piano needs repairing. Scholfield & Matthews have sent a man. Should I tell him to come up?'

This is it! she thought. Even at this moment, she couldn't make up her mind what to do. She stood silent, hesitating. She had to think of Gerald! I have to do it! she told herself. I have to! The jewels were insured, but at the back of her mind, she had a feeling that there was more to this than taking the old lady's jewel box. No one lives for ever, Bromhead had said and she remembered the bleak coldness in his eyes.

'Miss Oldhill?' There was a note of impatience in George's voice.

She had to do it!

She forced herself to say, 'Yes ... it's all right ... let him come up,' and with a shaking hand, she replaced the receiver. She closed her eyes.

He will gag and bind you. She would have to face a police investigation. This was madness. She couldn't go through with it! Then again her mind switched to Gerald; held prisoner with his life threatened!

Then two things happened simultaneously. The front doorbell rang and the telephone bell rang.

She started violently. She looked wildly to the front door, then down at the telephone. Because the telephone was by her hand and because she knew there was a thief at the front door, she lifted the telephone receiver.

'Yes?'

'This is Jack.'

Strength went out of her legs and she had to sit down.

'Sheila?'

'Yes.'

'It's off! I'll explain when I get back. Tell Harry it's off. We don't go ahead ... do you understand? Harry should be with you any second now ... tell him to go away. Now, listen, Sheila ...'

Then the operator on the hotel switchboard repeated her mistake. She pulled out the wrong plug and cut them off.

Standing before the front door of the penthouse, Harry had rung the bell. He waited. He heard no sound. Looking over his shoulder, he saw the elevator descend.

Ring once, Bromhead had said. Don't keep ringing as it will

136

alert the old lady. If she doesn't answer, she's lost her nerve. Walk down to the next floor. There's a fire escape staircase . . .

Harry waited another minute. Still the front door didn't open. So the stupid bitch had lost her nerve! He would make her sorry! A red cloud of viciousness filled his mind. Moving silently, he ran down the stairs to the 19th floor. As he disappeared around the bend in the staircase, Sheila replaced the telephone receiver and went to the front door.

She paused with her hand on the door handle. Suppose this man wouldn't believe Bromhead's message? Suppose he forced his way in? She slid the safety chain on the door into place, then she opened the door a few inches the chain would allow it to open. Her heart hammering, she looked around the door into the empty vestibule.

Was he standing against the wall . . . out of sight?

'Is – is there anyone there?' she asked huskily.

Only the faint hum of the ascending elevator answered her. She drew in a long, slow breath of relief. He had waited, become uneasy and had gone, she thought. She closed the door, turned the key and took off the chain.

As she did so, Harry leaned against the steel fire door, pushed and felt it give. He slid into Sheila's bedroom. He moved swiftly to the half-open door. He paused as he saw Sheila at the front door, her back turned to him. His thin lips came off his teeth in a snarl of viciousness. Silently he set down the little black bag. He would teach her! He looked at her long, slim back turned to him. A quick chopping blow would stun her. Then tape across her mouth. Then his fingers would dig into her body to teach her women didn't fool with him!

As he started towards her, Sheila turned and saw him. She saw his hands reaching for her. She saw the glitter in his little eyes. She knew something horrible was about to happen to her, yet she couldn't scream. Her throat was paralysed. As Harry struck at her, she slid along the wall. The side of his hand scraped her face.

'No!' she managed to whisper. 'You must listen!'

Harry snarled at her. He pulled himself together. His rage had upset his aim. This had never happened to him before. Always one chopping blow and he had had no further trouble. He had acted like a fighter, goaded, who swings a wild, stupid punch. He steadied himself and started again towards her.

The front doorbell rang.

Harry froze. He looked at Sheila who was backing away from

him. This was the unexpected that Bromhead had warned him about. He whirled around, caught up his black bag, slid past Sheila and into the living-room.

Sheila hesitated. She was shaking. The front doorbell rang again. Somehow she got control of herself. She unlocked the front door and opened it. The sight of the big, powerfully built man in a light weight grey suit came as a relief.

'Miss Oldhill?' The voice had a snap in it.

'Yes.'

'I'm Handley, hotel detective,' the man told her. 'I'm just checking. Sorry to bother you. Is everything okay?'

She hesitated, then said, 'Yes.'

Handley was staring at her.

Well, for God's sake, he was thinking: the woman with the blonde wig! What the hell was going on up here? He was sure. Blonde wig or no blonde wig this was the woman who had disappeared on floor 19.

He moved forward and Sheila gave ground.

'I understand, Miss Oodhill, you have a man here to repair the piano?'

'Yes.'

'Where is he?'

Listening to all this, Harry realized this was now a question of bluff. He appeared in the living-room doorway. Ignoring Handley, he approached Sheila.

'I don't understand it, miss,' he said. 'There's nothing wrong with the piano ... all the wires are fine. Do you think madam made a mistake?'

'I suppose she could have,' Sheila said huskily.

Harry shook his head.

'Well, there's nothing wrong with it.' He moved around Handley who was watching him to the front door. 'Mr Chapman will be along next month to tune it,' and he was out into the vestibule.

Handley went after him.

'Just a moment.'

Harry turned and stared inquiringly at the detective.

'What is it?'

'Let me look in that bag.'

'And who are you?' Harry asked mildly.

'House detective,' Handley said, aware that Sheila had shut the front door. He heard the key turn.

Harry opened the bag to reveal the tuning forks, the piano

tuning keys and the piano wires.

Handley was suddenly unsure of himself. He realized he could be putting himself out on a limb.

'Anything else, mister?' Harry asked and thumbed the elevator call button.

'What's your name?'

Harry's face hardened.

'Okay, brother,' he said. 'If you want to play it rough, I'll play it rough. Let's you and me go talk to Mr Lacey, your boss. Hotel dicks come a dime a dozen with me. So let's you and me go talk to Mr Lacey and I'll put in a complaint to my people. How's about that?'

The piano tuning equipment had thrown Handley. He knew he had no business being in the hotel at his hour. Lawson was on duty. Lacey would want to know what Lawson was doing. If this bastard got talking to Lacey, both Lawson and he could lose their jobs and he remembered this was the best job he had ever had.

The elevator arrived and the doors swished open.

'Go ahead,' Handley said. 'Forget it.'

Harry gave him a sneering little smile and entered the cage. The doors swished to.

Handley turned and stared at the front door of the penthouse. The woman with the blonde hair and the dustcoat! He was sure Lawson knew this woman was Sheila Oldhill and he had been bribed to keep his mouth shut. Handley decided he had better say nothing. He had been warned. Let Lawson handle this, he thought. Why walk into trouble?

He crossed to the second elevator and pressed the call button.

Patterson returned from the Board meeting and dropped into his desk chair. The meeting had gone on longer than usual. He was aware that the other members of the Board hadn't been impressed by his performance and he wasn't surprised. How could anyone concentrate on bank business with this thing hanging over his head?

Vera Cross came in.

'Chris ... Mrs Morely-Johnson has been on the telephone.'

Patterson stiffened. He felt himself turn hot, then cold.

'What did she want?' (As if he didn't know!)

'She sounded very cross. She said she was waiting for her will and you promised to bring it to her this morning.'

Patterson's heart beat so violently it was a long moment before he said, 'What did you say?'

'You were tied up with the Board meeting.'

'How did she take that?'

'She said she wanted to speak to Mr Fellows.'

Patterson flinched.

'Well ... go on!'

'I explained that Mr Fellows was also at the Board meeting. She said as soon as you were through to call her.'

Patterson eased his collar.

'Okay, Vera ... leave it for the moment. I have something to do.'

Vera looked at him, puzzled. She had never seen him look so pale or so worried.

'Is there something wrong, Chris? Anything I can do?'

Patterson wanted to yell at her to go to hell, but somehow he controlled himself.

'No ... nothing's wrong.' Even to him, his voice sounded strangled. 'On your way, honey.'

Bromhead had said: do nothing!

When she had gone, he pushed back his chair and got to his feet.

Now he *had* to do something! What the hell was Bromhead playing at? Patterson moved around his desk. Why wasn't the damned old woman dead? What was happening? What was he going to say to her? If he didn't call her, she would call Fellows, and Fellows would personally deliver the forged will to her. *Do nothing!* Patterson was now in a panic. His telephone bell buzzed. He stared at the telephone for a long moment, then he crossed to his desk and lifted the receiver.

'Mrs Morely-Johnson,' Vera told him. 'Shall I put her on?'

Patterson's mind skidded around inside his skull. Tell her I'm out? Tell her I'm ill? But he knew she would then ask for Fellows who would rush the forged will to her. Patterson knew he had to handle this. Somehow, he had to gain time.

'Put her on.'

He sat down.

'Chris?' Mrs Morely-Johnson's voice was even more raucous than usual.

'Good morning, Mrs Morely-Johnson. How are you?'

'Never mind how I am!' God! he thought, she's really in a mood! 'I've been waiting! You said you would bring my will this morning! It is now eleven-thirty. I will not be kept waiting!'

Dare he take a tough line? he asked himself. He could think of no alternative. He braced himself.

'I'm sorry,' he said and he put steel in his voice. 'I understood you to say the matter really wasn't all that urgent. I had to attend an unexpected Board meeting. It's because of these board meetings, Mrs Morely-Johnson, that I am able to turn over your holdings so profitably.'

How would she take that? he wondered, dabbing sweat from his forehead.

'When I ask for something, I expect to get it.' He was quick to note a slightly hesitant, slightly less hostile note in her voice.

'Of course. I do my best, Mrs Morely-Johnson.' Patterson realized he had made an impact. 'If you were behind my desk I think you would be a little more understanding if you will excuse me saying so. You are my most important client, but I have many other clients. Blame me if you will, but it is impossible to give you a completely exclusive service, as much as I would like to do so.'

There was a pause, then she said, her voice softer, 'That I understand. I know I am a demanding old woman. I guess I expect too much from you, Chris. My will is really nothing to do with you. I can't think why I'm bothering you with this. Now, Chris, you get on with your work and I'll talk to Mr Fellows.'

Patterson felt himself shrivel.

'I can't do that,' he said. 'It is my privilege to look after your affairs. May I come to see you at three o'clock this afternoon? I feel we should have a straight talk. It seems to me, Mrs Morely-Johnson, that you can't be satisfied with what I do for you. May we please discuss it?'

Jesus! he thought, now I really have stuck my neck out.

'Not satisfied?' Mrs Morely-Johnson's voice exploded against his eardrum. 'Now, Chris, I won't have you getting uppity with me! I'm an old woman and I won't be bullied! Then come here at three o'clock. We'll go into this ... and please bring me my will,' and she hung up.

Patterson sat back. Then this was the finish, he thought. He sat for a long moment, unable to think what he could do to save himself. Then slowly he got control of his panic. First, he must get the forged will from the legal department. He must get it and destroy it. With unsteady hands, he scrabbled through his papers and found the authorization Mrs Morely-Johnson had signed, then bracing himself, he went along to the legal department.

Irving Fellows was at his desk: a tall, thin, dehydrated man with steely black eyes and a balding head.

'Hi!' Patterson said, forcing his voice to sound cheerful. 'How's the kid?'

Fellows made no attempt to conceal his disapproval of Patterson. He lifted his shoulders.

'He's coming along, thank you. Do you want something?'

'Mrs Morely-Johnson's will,' and Patterson laid the authorization on Fellows' desk.

'Her will?' The heavy black eyebrows shot up. 'She had that three weeks ago and returned it.'

Patterson had got beyond the point of no return. He was in no mood to take anything from Fellows.

'So what? If she wants to look at her will every day for the next ten years that's no skin off your nose, is it?'

Deliberately offensive, Fellows studied the authorization, then handed it to his dowdy secretary.

'Get Mrs Morely-Johnson's will, please, and give it to Mr Patterson. Then looking at Patterson, he went on, 'Is she troubled by her will?'

'If you're all that curious,' Patterson said, 'why don't you call Mr Weidman? We keep her will: Weidman is the man to worry about it.'

That broadside silenced Fellows who glared at Patterson, then pulled a document towards him and began to study it.

Three minutes later, Patterson was back in his office with the forged will. One step forward! But he couldn't see how it would help him. Of course the old lady would have great difficulty in reading the will, but she would manage with the aid of her magnifying glass. She wouldn't ask Sheila nor himself to read it to her. He looked at his desk clock. It was just on 12.00. He had only three hours to come up with a solution. He sat, thinking. Finally, he decided there was only one way to get out of this mess. He would tell the old lady that his brief-case, containing the will, had been stolen from his car while he was having lunch. He felt sure she would accept this. Then a new will would have to be made. Then he thought of Abe Weidman.

There came a tap on the door and Bailey, the bank messenger, looked in.

'There's a Mr Bromhead asking to see you, Mr Patterson.'

Patterson controlled his expression only with an effort.

'I'll see him, Joe.'

Bromhead came in, his cockaded hat under his arm, his lean face bland, his bearing dignified. Looking at him, no one could have guessed he had raced back along the highway, driving the Rolls at exactly sixty miles an hour which was the official speed limit, never going over the limit, but tempted to, knowing the cops on this stretch of road could delay him if he went faster.

When Bailey had gone, Bromhead came to the desk.

The two men looked at each other.

'She's yelling for the will,' Patterson said, his voice unsteady. 'You told me to do nothing! What the hell are you playing at? I've got to take the will to her by three o'clock?'

'Here it is.' Bromhead produced an envelope from inside his tunic. He laid it on the desk. 'The original will, Mr Patterson. I would like the other.' He looked at the envelope lying on Patterson's blotter. 'Is that it?'

Patterson nodded.

'Yes, that's it.'

'I'm afraid, Mr Patterson, we are back to square A,' Bromhead said. 'Her nephew is dead.'

'Dead?' Patterson stared at him. His mind worked swiftly. The nephew dead, there would be no money for Bromhead nor for Sheila. This didn't bother him, but his own inheritance could still be in danger!

'We're not back to square A,' he said, his voice harsh. 'How about Weidman?'

Bromhead's stare made Patterson cringe. It was a look of a man regarding a small boy.

'Surely, Mr Patterson, you can handle Mr Weidman? May I make a suggestion? Tell him the old lady has changed her mind about the pictures. Old ladies often change their minds. It's not as if he can complain. The information you gave him was in confidence. I can't see why you should worry about Mr Weidman.'

Patterson drew in a long, slow breath.

'You mean it's all over . . . we really are back to square A?'

'I think you, Mr Patterson, can say it is over, depending on how you handle Mr Weidman. If you handle him well, then I would say it is just a matter of time before you become a rich man.'

Patterson's mind was darting this way and that. This sounded to him too good to be true.

'I want that tape,' he said.

Bromhead nodded.

'That I can understand, but what one wants and what one gets are two different things. The tape doesn't interest me. I don't have it. Miss Oldhill has it ... you should talk to her.' He picked up the forged will and regarded it. 'A pity: a lot of thought and work for nothing.' He slid the envelope inside his tunic, then moved to the door. 'Well, Mr Patterson, let us hope you will eventually become a rich man.'

Patterson stared fixedly at him, his mind busy. He said nothing.

When Bromhead had left the office, Patterson snatched up the telephone receiver.

'Vera ... get me Mr Abe Weidman,' he said.

In the private room of Chez Henri restaurant, Patterson waited impatiently for Abe Weidman to arrive. He kept looking at his watch as he toyed with his dry martini.

When he had called Weidman, Weidman had said it was impossible for him to have lunch. He already had a lunch date with a client.

'This is extremely urgent, Abe,' Patterson had said. 'It's something I must discuss with you. Couldn't you break your date?'

'What's so urgent about it?' Weidman had asked.

'It concerns you. We're talking over an open line.'

There was a pause, then Weidman had said, 'Okay, Chris, I'll be along at one-thirty ... Chez Henri?'

'That's right ... upstairs.'

During the drive to the restaurant, Patterson prepared his story. He now felt confident that he could handle Weidman, but he was worried about the tape that Bromhead had told him Sheila had. But one step at the time, he told himself. The tape would cost him money, but he was prepared to pay. He must try to do a deal with this woman.

Weidman came in.

'I'm sorry I'm late,' he said as he shook hands. 'I've had a hell of a morning and now you've certainly snarled up my afternoon.'

'I'm sorry, but this is important. What will you drink?'

'Same as you ... a double.'

Patterson gave the order.

As he sat down, Weidman looked searchingly at Patterson.

'What's it all about, Chris?'

'Let's order. Now you're here we may as well eat.'

The *maître d'hôtel* came in with the menus, followed by the waiter with the dry martini.

Weidman said he had a heavy afternoon of work. He wanted something light. He accepted the suggestion of asparagus, cold poached salmon and a tossed salad. Patterson said he would have the same.

Patterson talked about the Stock-market while the asparagus was being served, then when the waiter had left, he said, 'I'm worried about Mrs Morely-Johnson.'

Weidman bit into a stick of asparagus, reached for another and dipped it into the piquant sauce.

'Why?'

'I'm sorry to tell you, Abe, she has changed her mind about the new will.'

Weidman paused as he was about to convey the asparagus to his mouth.

'Changed her mind?'

'She has decided to revert back to her original will.'

Weidman sat back. His little black eyes were glazed with shock.

'Her original will?' His voice was strangled. 'You mean...?'

'I'm afraid so.' Patterson played with a stick of asparagus, not looking at Weidman. 'I saw her yesterday. She told me she had decided the Picassos should go to the museum. She said she had been thinking this over. She said as she hadn't told you, you wouldn't know, but she felt that the people of this town and the tourists would be reminded of her husband if she gave the pictures to the museum.'

Weidman put his asparagus back on his plate. Patterson looked up. He saw disappointment, shock and anger flit across the fat face.

'She's asking for her original will,' Patterson went on. 'She wants to give her new companion, Miss Oldhill, some money. She wants to make a codicil, but on the original will. I have it, of course. She told me to destroy the new will ... the one in which she left you the Picassos.'

'Goddamn it!' Weidman muttered. 'So I'm not to have the Picassos?'

A waiter opened the door, saw neither of the men had touched the first course, raised his eyebrows and quietly withdrew.

'Abe ... I know the old lady. She's a bit dotty,' Patterson

said. 'She could change her mind. I'm seeing her this afternoon. I still have the new will ... I haven't destroyed it. I want to give her time to change her mind. I know how much you have done for her in the past. If anyone deserves to have those pictures, it's you.'

Weidman rubbed his fat jaw.

'Old women! As you say, you just don't know what the hell gets into them. I ...' He broke off and raised his hands helplessly.

'I have some influence with her,' Patterson said. He leaned forward, looking directly at Weidman. 'I want to gain time. With a little time, I think I can talk her into giving you those pictures. I'm going to try if you will co-operate.'

Weidman stiffened and stared quizzingly at Patterson.

'What do you mean ... co-operate?'

'This is Friday. I've told her you are in New York until Monday,' Patterson said. 'This way I've gained time. She wanted to call you right away and get you to make the codicil. I'm sticking my neck out, Abe, but I feel confident this is an old woman's whim and I can persuade her to change her mind. If I've done wrong, you say so and I'll take the rap.'

Weidman began to speak, then stopped. He thought of the three magnificent Picassos on the walls of Mrs Morely-Johnson's vestibule. These pictures were something to yearn for. The thought of them hanging in the goddamn local museum was gall to his mind.

Patterson went on, 'She could still call your office. Give me a little time, Abe, and I think I can swing this your way.'

Weidman hesitated, but his sense of duty made him all attorney.

'We can't do this, Chris. I see you want to help and I appreciate it, but I can't go along with it.'

'Okay.' Patterson shrugged. 'I wanted to be helpful. Okay, if that's the way you feel about it. But I've told her you are in New York. Are you going to pull the rug from under my feet?'

Weidman shifted uneasily.

'I won't do that,' he said. 'No, I won't do that. Don't think I don't appreciate what you've done, but the old lady has the right to do what she likes with her pictures. I don't want to get involved in anything that could be ...' He stopped short, aware that Patterson was looking inquiringly at him. 'I don't want to get involved,' he ended lamely.

'I understand,' Patterson said. 'But I know the old lady. She blows hot ... then cold. You deserve these pictures, Abe. Let me try to handle this. Keep out of the way. If the old lady calls, tell your secretary to tell her you are out of town. Leave it until Monday. What's the harm?'

Weidman brooded over his untouched asparagus, his fat face dark with thought. He could only think of the three Picassos. Why not? It would mean only three days. Patterson might just swing it in his favour. It was worth a try.

He gave an abrupt little nod and picked up a stick of asparagus. Seeing him do this, Patterson knew he had made yet another step forward.

Just after midday, Bromhead drove the Rolls into the hotel garage. The Negro attendant who was washing a 280 Mercedes suspended his work and came over as Bromhead got out of the Rolls.

'Don't tell me you've been to L.A., Mr Bromhead,' he said. 'That sure would be moving.'

'I got half way there,' Bromhead said, ready with his story, 'then I knew what was wrong ... dirt in the carburettors. I stopped at a garage, they blew them out and she's going like a dream.'

The Negro giggled happily.

'What do you know, Mr Bromhead? Ain't that life?'

'That's it,' Bromhead said. 'I'll get me some lunch.'

'You do that, Mr Bromhead.' The Negro turned to admire the Rolls. 'Sure is a beauty, ain't she?'

'That's what she is.'

Bromhead walked to his room. He took the forged will from his tunic and put it on the table. He felt old and frustrated. It had been a good idea. It could have worked if that stupid Gerald had behaved himself and had stayed alive. Her only relative! He paused to look into his future. He would remain now the old lady's chauffeur. A cottage in Carmel was a dream like any dream. You woke up and found your dream was a puff of smoke. When she died, he would inherit $15,000 a year and the Rolls. With the high cost of living creeping up every year this sum would allow him to just tick over. It was a bleak prospect.

He picked up the envelope containing the will and tore it into small pieces, then carrying the pieces into the bathroom, he flushed them down the toilet.

Returning to the living-room, he called the penthouse.

When Sheila answered, he said, 'Jack ... how are you fixed?'

'She's recording,' Sheila told him. 'Come to my room.'

He took the elevator to the penthouse and let himself in with his key. He could hear Mrs Morely-Johnson playing ... Mozart? Beethoven? He didn't know. The notes had a liquid quality ... beautifully phrased. He went into Sheila's bedroom and found her standing at the window, waiting.

He closed the door.

'What happened?'

Briefly, she told him. She didn't tell him the whole truth. She said Harry had arrived and she had let him in, then the hotel detective had arrived. She said Harry had been clever in diverting the detective's suspicions.

So the unexpected had happened, Bromhead thought. Seeing it in perspective, he realized it was lucky the way it had turned out. He wouldn't have wanted the old lady to die if he couldn't profit by her death.

Now he had to break the news of Gerald's death. He had thought how best to do this. He wasn't sure how she would react. He had a growing suspicion that this dirty drop-out meant more to her than she had revealed. He didn't want a scene.

'Well, there it is,' he said. 'Things go wrong.' He paused, then went on, lowering his voice, 'I'm sorry ... I have bad news.'

She looked sharply at him.

'Bad news?'

'Gerald.'

Take it slowly, he told himself, break it gently. He saw her hands turn into fists.

'What about Gerald?'

'There's been an accident. I don't know how much Gerald meant to you ... I'm sorry ... he's dead.'

She recoiled.

'Dead?'

All the colour went out of her face and he was alarmed to see how shocked she was.

'I'm afraid so ... he died in a fire.'

'You killed him!' The sudden viciousness in her voice warned him how dangerous she could be unless he controlled her.

'No ... it was an accident.' He kept his voice low and calm. 'It was his fault.' His mind groped frantically for an inspiration to stop the scene he saw was coming. 'He was with a girl. They were on the top floor of a tenement building ... you know

Gerry. He was fooling around. The girl got scared and resisted him ... she was only a kid. He knocked over a lamp. The place went up in flames. They were both trapped.'

Watching her, he saw this was the right tactic. Her anger went away and she stared unbelievingly at him.

'A girl?'

'A teenager ... sixteen.' He dug in the dagger. 'You didn't expect Gerry to remain alone for so long without a woman, did you? He picked on this kid ... she was sixteen.'

Sheila flinched and turned away. She walked slowly to the window and rested her forehead against the pane.

'They both died,' Bromhead went on. 'That's why I called you. With him dead, there's no relative for the old lady to leave her money to ... we're back to square A.'

There was a long pause. Through the closed door came the magic sound of Mrs Morely-Johnson's piano playing.

After waiting several moments, Bromhead began to lose patience.

'I'm sorry, but after all he wasn't much.'

She turned, her smoky blue eyes alight and he knew he had said the wrong thing.

'Much? Who are you to judge? Do you think you're anything but a cheap crook?' The bitterness in her voice jolted him. 'To me, he was ... he was my husband!'

For a moment, Bromhead couldn't believe he had heard what she had said.

'What was that? He was your husband?'

'Go away!' She moved listlessly from the window and sat on the bed. She put her hands to her face.

Bromhead gaped at her.

'Yes ... we got married before we came here.'

'Gerry was your husband?'

Bromhead felt sweat break out on his face.

'Why didn't you tell me?'

'Why should I? You never asked. Go away!'

Bromhead thought of the forged will he had destroyed. He felt so frustrated he could have killed this woman sitting on the bed with her hands covering her face. His mind worked swiftly. There was still time. They still had Patterson in a trap. Harry was still in town. He could forge another will.

'Don't you realize, you fool,' he snarled, 'if you can prove you are Gerry's wife, you are his next of kin and all this money will come to you?'

She looked up. The dead expression in her eyes alarmed him.

'I don't want it!' she said. 'He's dead ... I thought I could make something of him ... with money. That's why I married him ... to have a hold on him ... I could have moulded him. He pretended money meant nothing to him, but I know better. He didn't understand its power. I could have taught him. Now ... he's dead ... I'm not interested in money.'

Bromhead controlled himself with an effort.

'You don't know what you're saying!' He couldn't keep his frustrated anger out of his voice. 'Forget him! You can always find some other boy ... what made that little creep so special? If you must have a lover half your age, you can always find one.' He knew he was saying things he would regret later, but he was so angry, he couldn't control himself. 'We can still swing this thing. I'll talk to Patterson. We'll try again. The money will go to Gerry's next of kin ... you! One million, five hundred thousand dollars! We can begin again!'

'Get out!'

The viciousness and the hatred in her voice shocked Bromhead. He stared at her, seeing the contempt and the hatred in her eyes and he realized further attempts to persuade her were useless, but he couldn't let so much money escape him without a supreme effort.

'Sheila! Pull yourself together! Listen to me...'

'Get out!'

The snap in her voice told him nothing he could say would make any impression. He wanted to hit her, but he controlled himself.

'All right ... then that's it.' He moved away from her. He couldn't resist hurting her. 'Gerry talked to me about you. He said you had a mother complex and you were a nut. He didn't give a damn about you, except when he had you in bed. That was all you were good for, he said. You are a nut, and you'll regret this when you're old – and that won't be long – unwanted and without money.'

'Get out!'

Bromhead accepted defeat. He left the room and made his way to the elevator. The living-room was alive with sound as Mrs Morely-Johnson's old fingers flew over the keyboard.

Left alone, Sheila sat motionless, her hands gripped between her knees. Mother complex? A nut? Yes, Bromhead was right. She had married Gerald because she wanted to be sure that when they got the money he wouldn't leave her for someone younger. He had been reluctant to marry. 'Why bother with this jazz?' he had demanded. 'Aren't we happy as we are?' But she knew she had to have a hold on him. With all that money involved, she had been confident she could have made something of him, but not if she hadn't some hold on him. He had been dependent on her for money. He had been happy to lounge about while she had provided for him. That had been her hold on him then. Bromhead's proposition had seemed to her then to offer the release she longed for: to be able to be with Gerry instead of slaving in the hospital, wondering all the time what he was doing: coming back tired, forcing herself to go out with him, trying all the time to be gay. Why had she done this? A nut? Yes ... there was this thing in her for the younger man. A nut was as good a description as anything. Now he was dead. She must be a nut, she thought, even to have thought of teaming up with a man like Bromhead. She supposed the thought of owning a million dollars had sent her off balance.

Well, now Gerry was dead. She thought back on her life. Doors opened, then closed. This was another door that had closed. She felt it was impossible to stay here any longer. She wasn't going to give up the rest of her life to wait on an old woman.

Then she thought of Patterson. He would remain smug, waiting for the old lady to die, sure of his inheritance. He was a man who thought only of himself. Suddenly she had a hatred for this man with his good looks, his confidence and his two-faced servility with the old lady. He mustn't get away with this! Why should he? Gerry was dead. She had nothing. Bromhead had nothing. Why should Patterson have anything?

'Sheila?'

Mrs Morely-Johnson was calling her. She got to her feet and went into the living-room.

'I'm going down to the grillroom,' Mrs Morely-Johnson said. 'I've just made another recording. Be a dear and label the box: Beethoven: Appassionata Sonata.'

'Of course.'

Mrs Morely-Johnson peered at her.

'Is your headache better?'

'It's gone.'

'I'm so glad.' She put her hand on Sheila's arm. 'Have a good lunch. Are you having something sent up?'

'Yes.'

'Have something nice. Mr Patterson is coming at three

o'clock. I intend to scold him. He's been quite cross with me.' She started slowly towards the front door. 'Would you see me to the elevator?'

Sheila looked at her, knowing this was the last time she would see her. She felt a pang of regret. The old, half-blind woman was not only a great artist, but she was kind. Kindness was something Sheila felt was without price. Until she had come to the penthouse, kindness to her was just a word in a dictionary.

She went with the old lady to the elevator. The attendant took charge of the old lady. He was an elderly man who would have given service even without Mrs Morely-Johnson's presents.

As soon as the doors swished to, Sheila went quickly to her bedroom. She opened the closet and took from it her two shabby suitcases. She packed quickly. Finished, she looked around the room, making sure she had left nothing behind that belonged to her, then satisfied, she opened a drawer in her dressing-table and took out the box, containing the *I, Christopher Patterson* tape.

She went into her office, found a biro and printed on the label of the box: Appassionata Sonata: Beethoven.

She went into the living-room. On one of the shelves of the bookcase were some thirty boxes of tape: all neatly labelled. She lifted some of them and inserted the box she had just labelled between them. Then she rewound the tape that Mrs Morely-Johnson had just recorded and put that in another box and left it unlabelled.

She went to her office. Sitting at her desk she wrote a brief note. Taking the note to her bedroom, she put it on her bare dressing-table. She looked around the comfortable room with regret, then shrugging, she put on a light dust coat, picked up the two suitcases and left the penthouse, leaving the key in the door.

As she was driven in a taxi to the bus station, she opened her handbag and checked her money. She had $95. She smiled a little bitterly. When she had arrived in this city, she had had $55 ... not a lot of profit, she thought.

At the bus station, she bought a ticket to Los Angeles. The driver stowed her two bags into the luggage compartment. The bus was half empty and she found a window seat. She planned to spend the night in Los Angeles and then take another bus to San Francisco. She was sure she would get a job easily enough at the Masonic hospital ... they were always short of staff. As she took a pack of cigarettes from her bag a young man sat down heavily by her side.

'Have you a cigarette to spare?' he asked as he squeezed a dirty duffle bag between his knees.

She looked at him: another Gerry, she thought. He was slim with hair reaching to his shoulders. His sun tanned face was pinched as if he ate badly. As he took the cigarette she offered him she saw his hands were dirty and his finger-nails black. She could smell his stale sweat.

They began to talk. After a while, when he began to loosen up, he sounded just like Gerry. He had the same stupid, youthful phrases: the scene must be changed! We have to get rid of the rich! There were too many old people! Gerry all over again. The usual destructive cant without suggesting anything constructive.

As the bus roared along the highway, she relaxed and listened.

She thought: He only needs a bath and some decent food. Maybe I could make something of him. He has good eyes.

When they reached Los Angeles, she suggested they should go to a hotel together. He stared at her, then grinned. She felt her blood move through her body as he looked at her with youthful lust.

As they walked together to the reception desk of a run-down, shabby hotel near the bus terminal, Gerry's ghost left her mind for ever.

Bromhead returned to his room. He opened a can of beer, poured the contents into a glass and then sat down.

Back to square A, he thought.

It could be worse. He would now have to accept a restricted future. The dream of the cottage in Carmel was just another dream. The old lady could last for years. When she died, he would have $15,000 a year. He must now be careful and save for the future.

Then suddenly he remembered Solly Marks. The thought of Marks brought him upright in his chair. He owed Marks $32,000. This sum could now never be repaid. He remembered Marks, staring at him as he said: 'I have a collecting service ... I thought I'd remind you.'

The possibility of some thug catching him when he was off guard and smashing his skull now became very real, but Bromhead never allowed himself to panic. This was something that had to be handled. He sat for some time, sipping his beer, while he thought, then coming to a decision, he reached for the telephone receiver. He caught Solly Marks just as he was leaving for a late lunch.

'Jack here,' Bromhead said. 'It's okay to talk. I'm on an outside line.'

He listened to Marks's wheezing breathing.

'I'm sorry about your problem,' Marks said. 'He set fire to the place. You can't blame me. I've lost a valuable tenement building.'

'I'm sorry about that too.' Bromhead paused, then went on. 'With my problem dead, Solly, the operation is dead. I'm calling to tell you to tear up those I.O.U.s I gave you.'

'That's something I never do,' Marks said, his voice turning hard. 'You pay or I'll have to collect and you know what that means.'

'You won't, because I have now an insurance policy covering me,' Bromhead said quietly.

There was a long pause while the line hummed and Bromhead listened to Marks's wheezy breathing. Then Marks said, 'What does that mean?'

'It means you tear up those I.O.U.s and you write off your loss as I am writing off my loss.'

'You think so?' There was now a snarl in Marks's voice.

'I know so, Solly, and I'll tell you why. Do you remember Harry Miller?'

'Harry Miller?' A startled note came into Marks's voice. 'I've heard of him.'

'Who hasn't?' Bromhead reached for his beer and took a sip. 'Harry happens to be a good friend of mine . . . I once saved his life. He wants to square things with me. He's funny that way. I've told him about your collecting service, Solly. He doesn't approve of it. If anything ever happens to me, Harry says it will be his pleasure to square it . . . do I have to spell it out?'

There was a long pause, then Marks said, a slight quaver in his voice, 'I don't know what you're talking about, Jack. Who said anything was going to happen to you?'

'Things can happen,' Bromhead said. 'Are you going to tear up those I.O.U.s, Solly?'

'Well if you haven't the money there's no point in keeping them, is there?'

'That's right. Okay, Solly . . . better luck next time if there's a next time,' and Bromhead hung up.

As Mrs Morely-Johnson didn't expect him back until 17.00, he decided to take Harry Miller out to lunch. It wasn't safe to bluff with Marks.

As he was driving to meet Harry, he considered his future. He, Harry and Marks were all around the same age. If Harry died first, he (Bromhead) would be in trouble for Bromhead knew Marks would never forget. If Marks died first, he (Bromhead) would have no more cares. If he died first, he would have even less cares.

It seemed to him his future now depended on how long Harry kept alive. It wasn't a very satisfactory outlook, but it was an outlook he had to accept.

At a few minutes to 15.00, Patterson entered the lobby of the Plaza Beach Hotel. He had come armed with a large box of marrons glacé which he knew Mrs Morely-Johnson adored. As he walked towards the elevator, George, the hall porter, intercepted him.

'Excuse me, Mr Patterson ... Mr Lacey would like a word with you.'

'Later,' Patterson said curtly. 'I have an appointment with Mrs Morely-Johnson.'

'It is to do with Mrs Morely-Johnson,' George said.

Patterson hesitated, then nodding, he went down the corridor leading to the Director's office.

Lacey got to his feet and shook hands.

'I felt you had better be warned,' he said. 'Mrs Morely Johnson is very upset. Her companion-help has left.'

Patterson stiffened. He stared at Lacey.

'Left?'

'While Madam was lunching in the grillroom, Miss Oldhill packed and left. She left a note.' Lacey handed a folded piece of paper to Patterson.

Putting down the box with its gay wrapping, Patterson unfolded the paper, aware his hands were unsteady.

He read:

Dear Mrs Morely-Johnson.

Forgive me for leaving like this. Please be understanding. Thank you for all your kindness. I won't be returning. Please don't think badly of me.

In sincere admiration.

    Sheila Oldhill

Patterson stared at the note, then making an effort to keep his face expressionless, he looked at Lacey.

'How extraordinary. So ... she's left?'

'Yes. She has taken all her things. Madam is very upset.'

'I'll go straight up.' Patterson put the note in his pocket. 'I'll have to find someone else to look after her. In the meantime, is there anyone...?'

'Of course. Maria has already been told. She's with her now.'

Picking up the box of marrons glacé, Patterson hurried to the elevator and was whisked to the penthouse. As the elevator rode smoothly up to the 20th floor, his mind was busy.

He could think only of the damaging tape. What had happened to it? Why had Sheila run off like this? Had she taken the tape with her? Was she planning to blackmail him? The Siberian wind was whistling through his mind.

Maria, the fat, kindly floor waitress, opened the front door. She looked worried.

'How is she?' Patterson asked as he entered the vestibule.

'Not too good, sir. She's on the terrace.'

Patterson braced himself and walked through the living-room and on to the terrace.

Mrs Morely-Johnson sat under a red and blue sun umbrella, staring sightlessly across the harbour. She sat with her hands folded in her lap and for the first time, Patterson realized how really old she was. She looked up, peering at him through her thick glasses, then she smiled.

'I don't know what I would do without you, Chris,' she said and held out her wrinkled, beautiful hand.

Patterson felt a stab of conscience. He bent over her hand and brushed it with his lips.

'Mr Lacey told me,' he said, putting the box on the table. 'This is the most extraordinary thing. She seemed so happy with you. I don't understand it ... it's extraordinary.'

Mrs Morely-Johnson lifted her hands and let them drop in her lap.

'I can understand it,' she said. 'She was too young. I think she was wise to leave. The old take strength from the young. It's just the way she left that has hurt me.'

'Yes.' Patterson sat down. 'I'm truly sorry. Shall I see if Mrs Fleming is still available ... you liked her, didn't you?'

'Yes ... I did. The old for the old.' Mrs Morely-Johnson again lifted her hands and again let them drop into her lap. It seemed to Patterson a gesture of defeat. 'Would you do that for me, Chris?'

'Of course.'

'There was something about that girl I liked so much,' she went on. 'You read her note. In sincere admiration. I think she really meant that.'

Patterson shifted uncomfortably.

'I'm sure she did.'

'Yes.' Mrs Morely-Johnson took off her glasses. 'She was kind to me. I will miss her.'

'I've brought you a little plesent ... marrons glacé.'

Mrs Morely-Johnson put on her glasses, leaned forward and peered at the box.

'And you are too kind, Chris.' Her hand patted his arm. 'Kindness is so rare. Thank you ... you will be rewarded ... you'll see.' She smiled at him.

Patterson felt himself shrivel.

'It's my pleasure,' he said huskily. 'I've brought your will.'

She waved her hands.

'It doesn't matter now, Chris. I'm sorry I was so tiresome about that. I wanted to reward her ... now she's left me. Take it back to the bank.'

Patterson thought of Abe Weidman. He would have to break the news to him that he wasn't going to get the Picassos. This didn't worry him. There was nothing Weidman could do about that. He would tell Weidman that he had tried hard, but he couldn't persuade the old lady to change her mind.

'I had better go at once to Mrs Fleming,' he said. 'If she is still free, I'll ask her to come this evening.'

'Would you do that? I'd be so grateful. I liked her. We should have chosen her in the first place ... Sheila was too young.'

'Yes.' Patterson got to his feet.

'Oh, Chris ...'

He paused. What now? His nerves were jumping.

'Yes, Mrs Morely-Johnson?'

'Would you be a dear and put on a tape for me? I'm feeling a little sad and my music helps me. Any tape will do. You will find them on the bookshelf.'

He looked at her, sitting under the sun umbrella, rich, old and lonely. These were the people he had to deal with, he thought. Old people! People who had the money!

'You mustn't feel sad,' he said gently. 'Why be sad?'

'Put on a tape,' Mrs Morely-Johnson said. 'You are young. You don't understand sadness.'

He hesitated for a moment, then went into the living-room and looked impatiently at the boxes of tapes on the bookshelf.

What had Sheila done with that tape? he wondered. Thrown it away? Cleaned it? Was she planning blackmail? He thought of the future days, the weeks and the months ahead while he waited for a telephone call. He took the top box from the pile, slid out the spool and threaded it on the recorder.

The clear, limpid notes of a Bach Fugue filled the living-room.

As he left the penthouse, he told himself that perhaps after all it would work out all right. Sheila had gone. Maybe she would forget him. What he didn't know, of course, was that the damaging tape, labelled *The Appassionata Sonata* had been within reach of his hand.

Sooner or later, Mrs Morely-Johnson would ask her next companion-help to put this tape on the recorder.

It was just a matter of time.